RELIEF | A QUARTERLY CHRISTIAN EXPRESSION

VOLUME ONE | ISSUE ONE

RELIEF | A QUARTERLY CHRISTIAN EXPRESSION

EDITOR-IN-CHIEF
Kimberly Culbertson

ASSISTANT EDITOR
Heather von Doehren

FICTION EDITOR
J. Mark Bertrand

CREATIVE NONFICTION EDITOR
Karen Miedrich-Luo

POETRY EDITOR
Brad Fruhauff

TECHNICAL EDITOR
Coach Culbertson

Relief: A Quarterly Christian Expression is published quarterly by ccPublishing, NFP, a 501(c)3 organization dedicated to advancing Christian literary writing. Mail can be sent to 60 W. Terra Cotta, Suite B, Unit 156, Crystal Lake, IL 60014-3548. Submissions are not accepted by mail.

SUBSCRIPTIONS
Subscriptions are $48 per year and can be purchased directly from the publisher by visiting http://www.reliefjournal.com. Single issues are also available.

COPYRIGHT
All works Copyright 2006 by the individual author credited. Anything not credited is Copyright 2006 by ccPublishing, NFP. No part of this publication may be reproduced, stored in a retrieval system, or transmitted by any means without prior written permission of ccPublishing, NFP.

SUBMISSIONS
Submissions are open year round via our Online Submisison System. Please visit our website at **http://www.reliefjournal.com** for instructions. Sorry, but we are unable to read or return submissions received by mail.

FOUNDERS

We thank the following people who, by subscribing or donating, have financially supported *Relief* as we launch the first issue:

WE OWE EXTRAORDINARY GRATITUDE TO OUR HEROES, WHO DONATED AT OR ABOVE $500:

HEATHER ACKMANN
THE MASTER'S ARTIST
http://www.mastersartist.com

AND ALSO TO THE REST OF OUR FOUNDERS, WHO HAVE HELPED US TO MAKE THIS JOURNAL A REALITY:

Our list of Founders will continue to grow after this issue has been printed. Additional Founders will be listed in Issue 2.

AOTEAROA EDITORIAL SERVICES
VASTHI ACOSTA
ADRIENNE ANDERSON
ELAINA AVALOS
SUSAN BOYER
JILL BERGKAMP
SUSAN H. BRITTON
SHAWN COHEN
CHAD COX
JEANNE DAMOFF
DIANNA DENNIS
STEVE ELLIOTT
CHRISTOPHER FISHER
DEBORAH GYAPONG
MATTHEW HENRY
GINA HOLMES
MICHAEL KEHOE

BILL AND PEGGIE KRUEGER
DAVID LONG
MANKATO
ANDREW MEISENHEIMER
CHARMAINE MORRIS
NANCY NORDENSON
KAREN T. NORRELL
RANDY PERKINS
SHANNA PHILIPSON
CALEB ROBERTS
CHRISTINA ROBERTSON
SUZAN ROBERTSON
LISA SAMSON
MICHAEL SNYDER
DOROTHEE SWANSON
AMBER TILSON
SHERRI TOBIAS

TABLE OF CONTENTS

FROM THE EDITOR'S DESK KIMBERLY CULBERTSON   6
EDITOR SYMPOSIUM   11
SAFE BOOKS ARE NOT A FOREWORD BY MICK SILVA   15

EDITOR'S CHOICE
ALL HEALED UP FICTION BY MICHAEL SNYDER   20
NOTHING CAN SEPARATE CREATIVE NONFICTION BY NANCY J. NORDENSON   28
SUNDAY SCHOOL LESSON POETRY BY JILL BERGKAMP   36

FICTION
REMOVED FROM HAZEROTH IVAN FAUTE   53
TURNER'S SIN J. MARK BERTRAND   63
MORTISE AND TENON CHAD GUSLER   68
A GAME OF HANGMAN RYAN J. JACK MCDERMOTT   93
AT THE REEF ALBERT HALEY   112

CREATIVE NONFICTION
ON CHILDREN, SEWERS, AND DICTATORS KIMBERLY GEORGE   47
BOOKSHELVES KAREN MIEDRICH-LUO   81
ZUGUNRUHE WM. ANTHONY CONNOLLY   126
HISTORY IN HER HAIR LISA OHLEN HARRIS   134
WRITING FROM THE INSIDE OUT LUCI SHAW   140

POETRY
ADVENT KRISTIN MULHERN NOBLIN   37
SILENCE KRISTIN MULHERN NOBLIN   40
BREATH OF WATER CHUCK BAKER   42
THE THROAT CHUCK BAKER   43
MOURNING PEGGY SMITH DUKE   44
MORE THAN THE BURN BRITTANY HAMPTON   45
STRICTER JUDGEMENT HEATHER VON DOEHREN   46
TWO SPIRITS DANIEL H. FAIRLY, JR.   57
SAMHAIN SHUFFLE (DANSE MACABRE) JERRY SALYER   58
HOW I EXPLAIN MY RELIGIOUS HISTORY AMBER HARRIS LEICHNER   61
CONVERSION MAUREEN DOYLE MCQUERRY   78
HOLLOWS MAUREEN DOYLE MCQUERRY   79
HOMING PIGEON MAUREEN DOYLE MCQUERRY   80

HYMN OF UNGRIEF ALLISON SMYTHE	87
THE WAY A DAY CAN BREAK ALLISON SMYTHE	89
HUNT THE THIMBLE ALLISON SMYTHE	91
EROTIKOS LOGOS SCOTT CAIRNS	104
HOMESTEADING IN PARADISE SALLY CLARK	105
THREE DAYS TRACI BRIMHALL	108
THE TASTE OF LOT'S WIFE TRACI BRIMHALL	109
IN THIS CONFESSIONAL KEITH WALLIS	110
DAWN BONNIE J. ETHERINGTON	111
GUTTING HOUSES NICOLE GORDY	122
RESTORATION OF THE CATHEDRAL DIANNE GARCIA	124
SUNDAY 2005 DIANNE GARCIA	125
LAKESIDE MASS CLAIRE MCQUERRY	137
SATURDAY MORNING BRAD FRUHAUFF	138
LAST THOUGHTS BRAD FRUHAUFF	139

COVER ART
THIS BEAUTIFUL COVER OVER ART PROVIDED BY ARS GRAPHICA. VISIT THEM AT **HTTP://WWW.ARSGRAPHICA.COM**

PLUS!
LOOK FOR A BONUS STORY, "LAST TRIP TO CRYSTAL MOON," BY R.M. OLIVER AT THE END OF THE JOURNAL. YOU'LL ENJOY THE PREVIEW OF *COACH'S MIDNIGHT DINER*, THE GENRE ANTHOLOGY COMING IN 2007 FROM CCPUBLISHING.

FROM THE EDITOR'S DESK KIMBERLY CULBERTSON
EDITOR-IN-CHIEF

I CAN'T THANK YOU ENOUGH FOR HOLDING THIS BOOK IN YOUR HANDS. Before you read the contents, though, it may be best if you know that this literary journal may not always color inside the lines or obey the rules many expect a Christian book to follow.

It is our goal to maintain honesty and authenticity in writing, and to that end I'll confess: This journal was born out of frustration. In a previous season of life, I served a tour of duty as an inner-city high school teacher. To say that I quit teaching to write would be a lie, but leaving teaching left me with a lot of unspent creative energy. For the first time in years, I could fully devote myself to writing, and I began to hash out my experiences in teaching and inner-city ministry on the page, and penned a few short stories that Mark, our Fiction Editor, would almost definitely have rejected. I was writing with the end goal of publication and began looking for a good fit. What I found, however, was not very encouraging—as a writer or a reader.

I began by surfing the web looking for places that offered support for Christian writers, and found quite a few. Many sites required that I sign a contract before posting which dictated what I could and couldn't write about—no sex, no swearing, no violence, no sin that isn't immediately punished, etc. I bristled under the constraints, thinking about all of the ways in which the requirements didn't fit with my understanding of either Christianity or good writing. I also discussed writing with a friend who was an MFA student, and he explained that spiritual writing was discussed with disdain in his program, and that the few who still made an effort toward "Christian writing" were viewed as somehow quaint. The Christian students had mostly given up on Christian writing; their experience was that secular journals looked down on, and sometimes directly prohibited, spiritual writing, while Christian venues were few and often wanted something easier and cleaner than they were willing to write. There are, of course, exceptions on both the Christian and secular sides of this equation, but the trends in both markets left a void for Christian writers who didn't want to write easy answers and sugar-coated realities.

As for reading Christian literature, the reason that many shop the Christian section—to be assured of a safe environment in which they know that the books will not offend them or challenge their picture of reality—is the same reason that most Christians I know avoid the section. Why read a book when there is no question which side it will come down on, who will win, whether the main character or his friend will be saved? Where is the sense of wonder? And how can I truly become immersed in a book if its depiction of reality has gang members shouting "Darn!" and "Fiddlesticks!" and then quickly getting saved? If the goal of many Christian publishers is to make sure that the most easily offended reader is safe by repainting reality in the books, they are bound to lose the average reader; I'm not easily offended, but I am easily bored.

In his foreword, "Safe Books are Not," Mick Silva discusses the slogan of a popular Christian radio station: "Safe for the whole family." The idea, as he mentions, is that if people listen to this station, they will not have to explain any "unsafe" content to their children. He returns that he doesn't mind explaining things to his children. While I can understand a certain amount of censorship regarding what we allow our children to see, hear, and read, it is frustrating to have this idea applied to Christian writing for adults. There are topics that adults should be allowed to read and discuss once they have put away childish things. Adults should not only help their children develop critical thinking skills, as Silva points out, but should be able to themselves employ that skill, even if it means putting down a book that offends them. The fact that so many authors have written to children, even in their adult books, has pushed many readers away from Christian writing.

As I continued working toward a book about my experiences in teaching, I found myself wondering where such a book would fit into the Christian literary world. The more I learned about the industry, the more discouraged I became. A book that doesn't paint gang bangers only as villains and Christians only as heroes, a book that deals with the grit of a school in which bloody fights happen daily, corrupt security guards are gang members themselves, and distorted sexuality is rampant would fit nicely onto secular shelves alongside many memoirs that tell similar tales of strength and beauty in the midst of violence and hardship—that is until it discusses how a Christian club interacts with those same students. The power of Christ cannot be written out of the story any more than the terrible truths of poverty, drug use, sexuality, and violence.

In the midst of these conversations and reflections came a quiet nudge from God to create this literary journal, which I'll admit I laughed off—until He whispered the name and I began to take the project seriously. With God's guidance, we're working diligently to create a venue for Christian writers that will allow for pictures of life that are sometimes beautiful, sometimes devastating, and always honest. We've asked writers not to pull their punches, and to send us their grittier work. The resulting stories, poetry, and creative nonfiction that you have before you craft a strong balance between worshipful moments that perceive God in nature and relationships, and sharp moments that still perceive God in pain and damage.

Not everyone will like the freedom we have given our authors. But before putting down the

KIMBERLY CULBERTSON EDITOR-IN-CHIEF

book, consider this: Jesus was never thrown off by sinners, and he did not pick perfect people to represent him when he was gone. He was not aghast at the adulteress, the prostitute, or the tax collector, but he openly ridiculed religious people who were caught up with the appearance of perfection, calling the Pharisees whitewashed tombs. Jesus wasn't concerned with outward appearances; he was concerned with inward motivations. It may be easier to follow a list of rules than to carefully gauge our hearts, but Jesus clearly calls us to do the latter. In our writing, we need to take honest looks at the characters, to allow them to be imperfect. Otherwise, we run the risk of becoming the pharisees, worrying about appearances and missing what Christ finds beautiful and valuable.

The Christian writing rulebook often doesn't have much room for imperfect characters though. For example, Heather, *Relief*'s Assistant Editor, posted her poem "Stricter Judgment" for critique on a popular writing site for Christians. The poem, which we've included in this issue of *Relief*, deals with a waitress who serves a group of Christians, receives a tract for a tip, and then swears under her breath. Having waitressed for many years, I can testify to the authenticity of this moment, even to the general dislike of Christians among waiters because of this type of behavior. As per the rules of the site, she bleeped out the forbidden word. It took some time before people figured out what had been omitted, but as soon as they did, the conversation was centered completely on that one word. One person even wrote something like, "That foul-mouthed waitress probably needed the tract more than the tip." It worked to her benefit that the information superhighway separated us. There was little discussion about the Christian characters who were oblivious to her needs or the biblical reference and layer of meaning in the name of the poem; the readers missed the point. This incident seems indicative of a larger problem with Christian writing—we worry about words, and we forget about people. Christ said that we should know his followers by our love for each other, not by our perfect behavior. So if you need to, brace yourself, because *Relief* deals with work that does not sugar-coat or windex reality. Instead we seek to publish and honor writers who are able to authentically express the realities of both life and Christ with exceptional craft.

In each issue, we have chosen to showcase a piece from each genre by honoring the author with the "Editor's Choice Award." Though choosing the winners was not easy, we offer our congratulations to Michael Snyder for his story "All Healed up," Nancy Nordenson for her creative nonfiction piece "Nothing Can Separate," and Jill Bergkamp for her poem "Sunday School Lesson." Snyder's story explores the underbelly of dishonest evangelical ministry and its effects on a young boy who is witness to it. A careful reader will see the power of a Christ that can push through the ache of betrayal, even the hallucinogenic effects of toad venom, to begin the painful process of healing. Nordenson's essay beautifully weaves two tragedies into one conversation, tracing her thoughts as she struggles to understand the realities of Christ in the face of death. Her piece recoils against the easy answers and clichés we often encounter when tragedy strikes, and her intimacy with despair and Christ leaves me tearful and awestruck each time I read it. Bergkamp's poem deals with the spiritual and sexual awakening of a young girl in a very "safe"

FROM THE EDITOR'S DESK

environment: Sunday School. The moment of epiphany is subtle but celebrates the beauty and melancholy of a loss of innocence which is necessary for a greater intimacy with God and a better knowledge of self. I hope that you'll relish the layered complexity of these three pieces.

We are also humbled and honored to present a fantastic line-up of work, including fiction by Albert Haley and Ryan J. Jack McDermott, Creative Nonfiction by Luci Shaw, Poetry by Scott Cairns, a foreword by Mick Silva, and much more. We are grateful to all of our authors for the priviledge of publishing their work.

There are many people who deserve thanks, but before I mention them, I'll thank the God of the universe who sent his son Jesus to rescue me from the tangled mess inside of me. God used the teachers at Willow Creek Community Church in this, especially John Burke, who taught the message that convinced me that Jesus, who I'd grown up hearing about, wanted a relationship with me, which I couldn't believe. Many thanks to Bill Hybels, John and Nancy Ortberg, Gene Appel, Mike Breaux, Randy Frazee, and Nancy Beach for their teaching over the past ten years. Though these people and others at Willow Creek have greatly influenced my life, they don't know me and are not responsible for the contents of this journal, so please don't send them hate mail about swear words.

We all owe a debt of gratitude to Ben (many of you know him as "Coach"). If I weren't married to a tech-savvy web wizard, the book you're holding would very likely be tied together with fancy ribbon. His confidence in me helps me to see all of what Christ has done in my life, and, well, I could go on, but he is my favorite part of reality, this side of heaven. Thanks also to Heather, who has been a true friend and has been both supportive of and essential to this journal, and to her husband, Alan, whose experiences in writing have helped to shape provided a valuable sounding board over the past year. To Karen, who was willing to jump into this adventure with me as our Creative Nonfiction Editor; to Mark, who I apparently, though unwittingly, bullied into his position as Fiction Editor; and to Brad, whose advice has always been sound, many years ago when he helped me to find God and now as our Poetry Editor: Thank you all for your hard work, patience, and prayers. None of this would be possible without you. We're grateful to their spouses, too—Alan, Brad, Laurie, and Katie—who gave them up for so many hours to allow them to be part of our adventure. To our authors: We are all humbled and honored by each submission we receive; thank you for allowing us the privilege of reading your work.

And finally, even though they didn't work directly on this journal, I'd like to thank the family and friends who have influenced me: my parents, Bill and Peggie Krueger who have always supported me in my endeavors, and whose love for me is unending; Grandma and Grandpa Krueger, who equipped me with my spiritual training wheels back in the day when toddler-Kim would run up to the altar while Grandpa was teaching; Ben's dad, Danny Culbertson, whose love and advice we cherish; and Christa and Ezequiel, our adopted family, whom we deeply love. There are friends who have stayed with me over years and years of ups and downs, who deserve unending gratitude: Karen, Dave, Jason, StevO, Amanda, Charmaine, Christy, and of course,

KIMBERLY CULBERTSON EDITOR-IN-CHIEF

Heather. To the people who have blessed my life for a season, especially my SHOC mentors—Alan, Chris, Mike, Eric, Dave V., Joyce, and Ken, waiters, fellow teachers, students, and most recently, Bible study friends—Mike, Beth, Eddie, Leslie, Jim, Lauren, Christy, and Bill, thank you thank you thank you.

And to our readers: Thank you and *enjoy*.

EDITOR SYMPOSIUM

Because this is our inaugural issue of *Relief: A Quarterly Christian Expression*, our editors have agreed to weigh in on some topics in order to help our readers and writers better know *Relief* and its staff. Enjoy.

HOW HAS FAITH INFLUENCED HOW YOU WRITE AND/OR EDIT?

HEATHER — On both the faith and the religion side, I'm quite new (within the past fours years). I'm a recovering atheist poet who used to perceive the Christian literary genre as being a sub par subculture. Upon salvation, I stopped writing, not knowing how to reconcile my new found faith with my previous notions. In fact, this journal marks my first attempt at creative writing since my conversion. Working on Relief has provided me with, well, relief. As an editor, I am humbled by how many writers genuinely strive to produce writing that challenges. As both a writer and an editor, I am challenged by how to remain truthful and non-judgmental.

BRAD — I have a temperamental inclination toward cynicism which can teeter close to despair, and this can impact my expectations for myself and others. Faith critiques cynicism and finds the face of the other in the work, whether I think it good or not.

KAREN — Faith is a word shadowed with meanings. For purposes of this question I'll stay close to the definition of faith as trust in God. For although my belief in God remains constant, my level of trust wanes and flourishes depending on just about everything I encounter. I don't always understand the ways of God. I rarely grasp the why. But since my belief is firm, I want to try. When Paul says: I want to know Him and the fellowship of His sufferings, I have to ask why. I hate pain. As a nonfiction writer and editor, I strive for that Pauline kind of transparency and a means of plumbing the depths of murky waters. Writing, more than any other art, engages me in that quest. It is a means of searching the heart, exposing the truth, feeding the soul. When writing does this, and does it well, then I am satisfied.

MARK — Over time, it's impressed on me the seriousness of craft—not just the message of art but the way one goes about making it. That pushes me, as a writer, toward increasingly difficult, layered work. As an editor, though, I've come to respect the way these influences shape us all in different ways. I'm not looking for stories that fit my vision of the world so much as I'm hunting for fiction that communicate somebody else's, that shows me what their beliefs really mean to them. I guess you could say that faith breeds a confidence that's willing to entertain alternate conceptions of faith.

COACH — I like Jesus—Yay, Jesus.

EDITOR'S SYMPOSIUM

WHAT DO YOU HOPE *RELIEF* WILL ACCOMPLISH IN CHRISTIAN WRITING?

HEATHER — I hope that *Relief* provides a place, free from restraints, for writers to portray all aspects of what it means trying to be Christian in today's world.

BRAD — *Relief*'s ideal authors are already out there; they are serious, thoughtful Christians who believe that neither God nor faith are "safe," and that literature can both remind us of that and help us understand it. I only hope we can become an important forum for their voices.

KAREN — Many Christian writers spend so much time focusing on what they hope for in life, so much effort trying to create an imaginary paradise in order to comfort themselves and others, that their work bears little resemblance to the stark beauty found in the real world. Those who manage to see the Transcendent in say, a prostitute, are often marginalized to avoid offending the reading public. I have a hope that *Relief* will give writers a place to explore their art without fear of giving offense. I am not talking about writers pushing boundaries or using shock value to stand out from the crowd, but instead about entering into a creative process with the Supreme Creator and doing it with excellence and with honesty. I would like for the non-Christian reader to thumb through the pages of *Relief* and be sucked in by that excellence and honesty.

MARK — I want *Relief* to prove two things. First, that engaging literary fiction can be written from an honest Christian perspective. Second, that there are people prepared to read such stuff. There are a lot of people, on the one hand, who think that today's Christianity is antithetical to fine art, and a lot of people on the other who think Christians are dimwitted and can't read above the fifth grade level. I'd like to do our part in proving them both wrong.

COACH — There are many elements that are suspiciously missing in Christian writing right now, namely ninjas and aliens. I'd also like to see a few more drunk detectives, and maybe some drunk detective ninja monkeys. That ride in spaceships. I believe that Jesus was a party guy, too. At the Cana wedding, he made wine, and good wine at that. Though genre fiction is not likely to show up in the pages of *Relief*, I'm hoping that the journal will not only add authenticity to Christian writing, but also some good old fashioned fun along the way.

EDITOR'S SYMPOSIUM

AS YOU WERE READING SUBMISSIONS, IS THERE A PIECE THAT STAYED IN YOUR THOUGHTS LONG AFTER READING IT? WHY?

HEATHER — Yes, both Jill Berkamp's and Traci Brimhall's poems had that effect days after reviewing them. I found that the more I scrutinized the pieces, the more I saw. Each time I returned to these poems, I was stunned at how each author could compact so much into such a tiny package.

BRAD — Honestly, there were a few, and for many different reasons. But those by Bergkamp, Cairns, McQuerry and Noblin all stuck out for what I think of as a sacramental or incarnational sensibility, a perception of the numinous in the material. (But don't everyone go sending me all poems just like those.)

KAREN — I was especially drawn to Nancy Nordenson's piece about the suicide of a friend. It's a terribly difficult subject to write about without affectation or trite answers or despair. When she juxtaposed her own personal trauma within the piece and came away from both experiences with a reverence for God, it moved me to tears—every single time I read it or edited it. (I rarely cry more than once over something!) It is very wonderful writing.

MARK — That was pretty much my criteria for selection. I latched onto stories that captured my attention, stayed with me and cried out for second readings. The fiction in this issue is not just readable—it's re-readable. I've poured over these sentences and grown possessive about them. People picture editors as grim-faced Victorian gentlemen wielding red pens, but reading submissions is more like speed dating. You do it with an open heart, hoping to fall in love. In this case, I did. Five times.

COACH — We've received several genre pieces in the mix along with the more "literary" work, but most of the pieces that I loved just didn't quite fit into *Relief*. So I said, "Hey, let's do a genre anthology, too," and everybody said, "Yay!" At the end of the journal, you'll find a promotional piece for the upcoming *Coach's Midnight Diner*. "Last Trip to Crystal Moon" deals with a tattooed bouncer at a strip club. It's a strong story about doing the right thing, even when the right thing isn't quite acceptable either.

EDITOR'S SYMPOSIUM

THANK YOU:

HEATHER   To my parents, friends, and my dear husband Alan, thank you for all your love, support, and guidance. To Kevin Stein and the good folks at the University of Arkansas, thank you for teaching.

BRAD   My wife, Katie, who has with longsuffering endured yet another time-consuming activity in my schedule; my family, who used to say I could be a writer— or a lawyer; my editor, who has been flexible with deadlines; my wife, who chose a career that can financially support the one I chose; God, who arranged a chance meeting with Kim in Grand Rapids, MI, and who you're expecting me to thank anyway; and my wife, whose heard enough about this project to be another editor.

KAREN   To the staff at *Relief* for putting your all into this journal and giving authors and subscribers a work of true excellence. Thank you to my private critique group (you know who you are.) You guys are the artists that I strive to be and your honest critiques, unflagging encouragement, commitment to skill, even your own personal work are a constant motivation to do my best. Finally, thank you Brad, Hannah, and Bethany, for allowing me the privilege to do what I love. You are the three muses, a constant source of inspiration and desire.

MARK   Do you thank people who get you involved in a literary magazine, or stop talking to them altogether? It's a dilemma. But I'll start by thanking Karen Miedrich-Luo for putting me forward and Kimberly Culbertson for not taking no for an answer. And I'm grateful to my friends at *The Master's Artist*, a group blog for Christian writers, who have been supportive of the project since the beginning. Naturally, I want to thank the writers who've submitted their work to us—whether we've been able to use it or not. There are a lot of voices out there struggling to be heard, and it's a pleasure to be able to give a few of them this platform. Most of all, I thank my wife Laurie for putting up with the long hours, for being a sounding board, and for her constant support during this new adventure.

COACH   I'll thank my dad, who taught me to step up, my Aunt Elaine for teaching me to stand out, my Mom for forcing me to extend my definitions, Dave Brumbaugh for being both a teacher and a student, my second grade teacher Mrs. Roberts for encouraging me to write, my adopted kids Christa and Zeke who showed me the ability to persevere despite all circumstances, and my wife Kimberly who stands with me through everything. And Yeshua Ben David, who showed us all that a perceived failure is never the end.

SAFE BOOKS ARE NOT A FORWARD BY MICK SILVA

7:23 pm. WaterBrook Press Corporate Offices, Colorado Springs

Publishing can be so infuriating. No surprise, really, but some days it's a million miles from the rosy-hued, soft-lit glam shot I held in my mind in college. That magical dance of professional editing, capturing and liberating brilliant beauty and intriguing insights. The mythic fight for truth and beauty within my essential and glorious task.

I should have stayed in film school.

But making books seemed so interesting. A worthy process of sorting through words to find those most book-worthy. I knew there would be opposition. But I guess I didn't expect it to be everywhere.

I've run into a major barricade. Actually, it's happened so many times, I wonder if there's even a way around it. It seems pervasive and particularly Christian—maybe even characterizing the entire subculture. It's caused difficulty in my work, so I'm hereby excoriating it as a formal theory. I've known about this scandal for a few years, its symptoms popping up in various areas, but never really recognized the scandalous little bug that caused it.

The theory:

Safe often equals shoddy.

Now obviously, "often" is an important caveat here. Establishing this as a law would be hasty. But take the statement as its own example. The word *often* in that phrase is a qualifier, reducing its simplicity. Its appeal, and even its usefulness, is also reduced. Without the word it may still be true, but we can't take that chance. We have to accept the sacrifice to the phrase rather than risk the stronger statement.

Or do we?

I've seen this theory proven a lot. Take toys for example. Old toys have all kinds of fun, dangerous qualities: sharp edges, metal pieces, long cords, choking hazards. Compare them to the lame, plastic spongy thingies today. It's nearly impossible not to feel sorry for kids who won't ever get to damage their innocent dignity on a rusty old hobbyhorse. Or take nature itself: nature isn't safe. You could die in the wilderness. But a brilliant orange sunset over a snow-capped mountain could almost kill you with its beauty.

So I have to wonder, do we fear beauty? My three-year-old daughter was listening recently to a tape of Disney movie songs. Some of them are so sweet they break your heart. They're meant to. When I came in the other night, she was crying. "What's wrong, honey? You don't like this song?" I moved to turn it off. "No, Daddy." She motioned for me to sit. "It's pretty. It's just so sad." Instantly I realized my instinct to rescue her. She was crying and I didn't like it. I feared her pain, but she wanted to feel it. To her, it was beautiful.

Safe things (there's that word again) often presume a consideration of children. A Christian radio station here claims to be "safe for the whole family"—assumedly because I shouldn't have to explain anything to my kids. But I like explaining things to my kids. Kids want their view expanded, their little eyes opened. Obviously, there's a maturity level to consider; no one needs to experience certain dangers. But risk brings awareness. Protecting readers dilutes the excitement of facing our natural fears. A window opens on a previously hidden truth and our reality grows.

It's been a while since the Christian Booksellers Association (CBA) released their report on the "critical issues" facing Christian bookstores. When I saw that the report included the need for "a safe shopping environment" among the half-dozen issues listed, I went and looked up the word safe in the dictionary. Two are worth mentioning here:

> 1. *unlikely to cause or result in harm, injury, or damage.*
> 2. *cautious with regard to risks or unforeseen problems, conservative with regard to estimates, or unadventurous with regard to choices and decisions.*

These definitions certainly fit the Christian book industry. Being raised in the church, I myself struggle against this mindset: "If our works aren't pretty, at least they're safer than the alternative." Unfortunately, that's not true. By aiming for safety, (pesky word again) Christians can create the most offensive works around. Ironic, isn't it? What would happen if we ditched some of our notions about safety? What would we find? What if we stopped trying to avoid danger and instead worked at writing from the foundation of wholly connected lives? What discoveries might we find?

I think abandoning safety is ironically a "safer" way to write. I've proposed renaming Christian books "God's books" before, but now I've got a better idea. "Books for God" seems clearer. No, they're not books for Christians. They're books for God. That's why Christians read them. If a bunch of us started using that term, it might start a little grassroots movement.

I think it's time to distinguish ourselves from the unsavory connotations of Christian books. Some might be confused, at first, but it could raise the opportunity to discuss the term and why we changed it.

Are books for God different from Christian books?

Maybe there isn't anything unbiblical in the way our current Christian culture is producing books. Maybe it isn't a problem that the ideal has become a clean, tame pond pooled from God's raging sea of wild creation. Maybe we shouldn't worry that we've mitigated the majesty and made "Christian" a mere adjective. If Christian writers (i.e. writers for God) are forced to twist their books into barricades against those who can't divorce art and message, maybe that's an acceptable alternative to facing reality's evil.

But all those maybes don't explain why challenging that viewpoint draws your faith into question.

Maybe God is bigger than our maybes can currently allow.

I'm hopeful for books that challenge Christians to spend time with messy creation. Maybe that's an unsafe topic God would have us explore. If we could get past our safe maybes we might produce works of higher quality. And maybe we'd be more effective at finding how to love and accept our world as well.

So I freely confess that I'm hopeful for writers who are passionate, full of the spirit, and trusting of the inherent goodness of their gifts. I believe it's important to confront this altered view of Christianity we've accepted where safe havens of adequate and mediocre can fester and breed. I'm hopeful for well-crafted books that don't bar the doors on the dangerous world and show us the rewards of taking risks for beauty. I want books that tell the safety-lusters to take a fresh look at Jesus before they judge the riff-raff he hangs out with. I want stories that reveal not a safe buddy or a nice friend, a happy hippie or a haughty holy-man, but a true, scandalous Jesus who had a rough reputation at the temple. It's time for metaphors that show his choice of the street corners over the safe havens.

Writers for God, it's time to honor your vigor for truth and beauty. Keep in mind that God doesn't ask us to preach holiness, in our lives or in our books. So keep quiet about your personal commitment and avoid alienating those with less-than-beautiful books. But for ourselves, we must accept the full creative palate of the world's contrasting colors. We must stop expecting readers to clean up their acts before welcoming them to our books. We must stop cleaning up the world before we present it to our readers.

I believe it's time the books-for-God industry remembered that love is more important than safety. Our need for books that don't offend has led to works of diluted, distorted reality. If our books offend, let them offend. Let's welcome in the riff-raff. It's time to stop insulating ourselves for narrow-minded readers. No more compromising to write sanitized books that don't attract Jesus's people.

Do we love others more than safe books? Can we unlock the door to the world around us?

Is it more than a dream or does your heart beat with this too?

Our books must strive to bear the full weight of truth and beauty to illuminate and honor our inspiration.

But first, as writers for God, we must give up the delusion of safety.

MICK SILVA *spent five years as editor and writer for Focus on the Family Resources before reinventing himself as an acquisitions editor for WaterBrook Multnomah. He is a summer on the skin-tone wheel. Recently, he made the switch from oval-shaped to decidedly-unsafe rectangular frame reading glasses, which really do seem to make him look smarter.*

RELIEF | A QUARTERLY CHRISTIAN EXPRESSION

CONGRATULATES THE WINNERS OF ITS

EDITOR'S CHOICE AWARDS

<u>FICTION</u>

MICHAEL SNYDER

ALL HEALED UP

<u>CREATIVE NONFICTION</u>

NANCY J. NORDENSON

NOTHING CAN SEPERATE

<u>POETRY</u>

JILL BERGKAMP

SUNDAY SCHOOL LESSON

ALL HEALED UP MICHAEL SNYDER

"Kill the toad, man. Before it kills you."

That was the last thing my record producer ever said to me. He didn't die or move away or anything. Like everyone else I know, he just got fed up and stopped talking to me. That was four years ago. I've been driving ever since.

My current travel companion smells like yeast and somebody else's cigarettes. His name begins with a K but I gave up trying to remember it about a hundred miles back. I picked him up on I-65 at sunrise and he hasn't stopped picking paint flecks off his jeans since, slipping them into a zippered pouch on his backpack. Had to ask him twice to stop singing. And I suspect I'll either have to keep asking or shut the radio off. He's telling me his story, how he wound up thumbing rides in the middle of August, casting blame like breadcrumbs. Problem is, he still believes he'll find his way home, oblivious to the defeat in his own eyes and the fact that he's already booked passage on the orphan train. If not for a brainless supervisor, a lazy ex-girlfriend, a dismal zodiac reading, and some uppity negro named Tayshawn, my new friend would be the mayor of earth. His life is everyone's fault but his. You can hear him working his tale out in fits and starts, repeating parts with added fervor, as if convincing me will somehow make it true.

He must realize his story's out of gas so he decides to involve me. "So, Jeremy, is it? What do you do for a living?"

"You're looking at it," I say, eyes still on the road.

"That's it, you just drive?"

"Pretty much."

"Jeremy the driver, eh?" A few seconds pass in silence, then he cocks his head like an overly curious basset hound. "So, you like an escort driver or whatchamacallit? A courier?"

I consider his original question again, vaguely aware of the underwater effect of heat shimmering on asphalt. What exactly do I do for a living? The question implies an exchange of some kind, a sacrifice maybe. But I don't ask for much and I forfeit even less. I'm a nomad. Gas stations and ATM's are my oases. And I've narrowed my addictions to exactly one. So I don't really do much of anything. I'm not even sure what I do do actually qualifies as living.

K obviously reads too much into my silence. He snaps his dirty fingers and says, "I shoulda known, man. You're running dope, aren't you? Or is it guns? Just my friggin' luck, hooking up with a damn drug smug—"

A familiar turbulence works its way through my system. I recognize the sound first, then the emotion. Laughter. My body and my brain are wracked with it. And when I realize how long it's been since the last time, I laugh even harder. I can't stop. Hell, I can barely drive.

The spasms subside when I narrowly miss sideswiping a tractor-trailer, sobering me up enough to make the exit and park alongside an antique gas pump. K is out of the car and heading toward the convenience store, either afraid or offended or both.

If he only knew how close to right he was.

I GAVE MY SISTER CANCER when we were nine. The adults in my world tried to convince me otherwise, but I knew what I knew.

The leaves were browning and the air reeked of exhaust from a nearby tire factory. I was Peter and she was Tinker Bell, dueling imaginary pirates when I knocked Katie out of our tree fort. The ambulance carted her off with a broken collarbone. She came home three months later with leukemia and died six months after that, on our birthday. We shared the same womb. She got the looks and brains. I got the attitude and all the healthy cells.

The shrinks talked about displacement, said that I was transferring blame and withdrawing to a dangerous place. Katie called me a silly boy for blaming myself, said that we were lucky that the broken collarbone helped them find the cancer so that God and Daddy could get her all healed up. That's what she'd say, all healed up, with a pink-and-green inflection that made you believe it. I loved her even more for that.

We buried Katie two days later, along with the best of what was left of our family. My mother pretended that nothing happened. My father quit meeting my eyes. My brain told me I killed my twin sister.

Eventually they tried to replace Katie with a new baby. But it felt cheap, like buying a new hamster because the dog ate the last one, as if affections were disposable. Turns out, maybe they are.

Tink lost her light. Peter grew up, bitter and filled with regret.

* * *

I'm a little surprised when K-man returns from the men's room, munching a Slim Jim and sipping chocolate milk. He leans one shoulder on the truck, trying to look casual but missing badly. It's obvious he's anxious about something but can't figure how to broach the subject. Another attempt at small talk fizzles on his tongue so I point the neck of my Coke bottle at the tarp-covered truck bed and say, "Feel free to have a look around. Might put your mind at ease."

His neck turns pink and his hands fly up, miming surrender. "Hey, you say you ain't carrying shit, then I guess you ain't carrying any."

He climbs back into my truck and I follow. Once we reach cruising speed I say, "Just to be clear, you know I never really said that." I watch his eyebrows flirt with his hairline. "You know, that I wasn't carrying."

His face and hands morph into the sign language equivalent of say what?

I shrug and hit the seek button on the radio. His fidgeting turns chronic and his eyes scan every crevice of the cab. He scratches phantom itches and keeps stretching his back to mask his curiosity. The radio dial pauses to preview the strongest signals, teasing us with snippets of rap, country, talk, metal, and sports until I hear an all-too familiar voice. As it too disappears, K's hand shoots forward. "Go back, man. I love that tune."

I manually crank the digits back until the familiar voice returns, my voice from another lifetime. For once I don't ask him to quit singing.

The assumption early on was that I would follow in my father's lucrative footsteps. Lord knows I had the training. In the early days, Dad used to make Katie and me travel with him to hick towns all over the Southeast. He'd drop us off at the local ice cream shop with a pocketful of quarters while he drove to the big tent to begin his reconnaissance, shaking hands, praying, re-inspecting his hair, and choreographing the transitions between music, healings, and offering plates. Katie and I would mingle with the hordes of religious nuts, cripples, and thrill seekers before taking up our posts on the front row. Our job was to feed the kitty, to prime the pump, to get the ball rolling, or any number of clichéd synonyms for warming up the crowd. "Nobody likes to go first," he'd say, as if our pretending were perfectly normal. "You two are like movie ushers for the Holy Spirit." I hadn't learned the word pimping yet. With Katie as my escort, I hobbled and grimaced onto the stage. After receiving my holy antidote, Katie would grab a microphone and testify to my previous afflictions and subsequent healing.

Dad eventually graduated from backwoods revivals to local religious programming, and from there to a national platform—the higher the profile, the more conservative the ministry. Once he massaged his Katie testimony into tear-inducing spectacle, he gave up the healing routine altogether.

When I was fifteen I worked up the courage to challenge him on this.

"Don't you think it's... I don't know, sacrilegious... to use Katie's death to make money?"

"Is that what you think this is all about?" He looked shocked, hurt even. "Son, your sister's death is the single worst thing that's ever happened to me. But it's like, like a casualty of war, unfortunate but necessary. It wreaked havoc on our lives, but God is using it for a greater good. Just like He's going to use you."

"You can tell God to keep his grubby hands off me."

Dad smirked and shook his head. "You're just like the Pharaoh, son. Your heart is as hard as your head—and that's saying a lot. But mark my words, God is going to use you whether you sign up for eternity or not."

"You mean like how you used us? In your healings?"

Dad flinched. He made a fist and I think he meant to use it. Instead he showed me his back, feeding the murder in my heart.

From that day forward my religion became the formation of a new self, the antithesis of my father, pursuing every god but his, indulging every whim into a fresh addiction. I moved in with communists, overdosed on jazz, and slept with blacks and Mexicans. Even forced myself to learn to write left-handed. The outlet for my cancerous existence was music, my own gritty brand of alt-rock. Rolling Stone christened me "an angry poet for a legion of disenfranchised misfits." But I still couldn't escape my father's shadow. Art was not enough. I needed fame, too, if for no other reason than to rub my father's nose in it. Somewhere along the way I sabotaged my career, my passion, my one good gift, all for the empty pursuit of glory. I turned into the thing I hated most.

THE TENNESSEE STATE TROOPERS ARE OUT IN FORCE, tucked into blind spots on the median. The sight of them cranks on K's curious fidgeting like a ratchet. His demeanor has sunk to just south of paranoid.

"You okay?" I say. "You don't look so good."

"I'm fine, man. I'm fine. I mean, well, on second thought I guess I could use a tissue." He leans forward and opens the glove box, then yelps like a little girl when Prince jumps into his lap.

"Calm down," I say. "You're gonna scare him."

"Get him off me." K tries mightily to shrink away from the hideous fist-sized toad resting on his thigh. "I think he freakin' peed on me."

"I think he thinks you peed on him."

K's feet keep backpedaling uselessly on the floor board until I scoop Prince into my own lap and caress his knobby brown flesh with my thumb. He blinks at the panting man in the passenger seat.

* * *

I was sober when Amanda told me she loved me—not a good combination at all.

"Wait," I said. "You're serious, aren't you?"

Eyes glistening, she bit her lip and nodded.

"We had a deal, remember?"

"What, you don't think I know about you slipping out at night for cheeseburgers?" She meant this to be funny, making light of our ground rules—no hard drugs, no meat, and no falling in love. But it just hung there between us. Until the first tear fell, clearing tracks for others. I could never stand the way she looked like Katie when she cried.

"You know," I said. "That is the single most unattractive quality I can think of."

"What? Crying? Or the ability to actually fall in love with someone?"

"No, falling in love with me. I could never respect you for that."

That same afternoon, I drove past public restrooms until I could hear her bladder scream for mercy. When she duck-walked into the ladies' room at a rest stop in Colorado I crammed two thousand dollars and a hand-written note into her purse and gave it to the security officer at the information desk. The note said "Sorry."

And I was.

That was 2002, the winter I spent with the hippies. These were the real hippies, the grow-your-own types, Manson family throwbacks, free love enthusiasts, not the rich kids with smelly dreadlocks, $300 sandals, and corporate-sponsored jam band festivals with working toilets. They adopted me into their community as one of their own. It didn't hurt that I had money. Or that I evened out the guy/girl ratio. Or that I was half their age. Or that I was a bit of a celebrity.

We practiced a nightly ritual which included bonfires, guitars and tambourines, reefer, and something they called "The Chosen One," although I never observed any actual choosing. It was more of an even rotation. When his or her turn came up, the chosen one would select from an assortment of modified crack pipes, load it with what looked to be flecks of dried paste, and begin leisurely toking.

By the time the hallucinations commenced in full, we were all primed with marijuana and ready for a show. And the chosen one rarely disappointed. Our communal intoxication left us with the profound impression that we'd finally partaken in something real.

After my third stint as the chosen one, I left $500 in the community money bag and snuck out of camp with Prince and a handful of loaded baggies.

We find an abandoned campground at the base of the Smokey Mountains. It turns out that

K is less jumpy when given a job to do. He doesn't talk any less, though, recounting his mother's battle with lung cancer and her subsequent memorial service in excruciating detail while he twists a can opener around a can of baked beans. He's done most of the work, as I'm too anxious to help. Tonight I'm the chosen one.

We devour multiple helpings of sausage and beans while the gray sky fades to black and the forest chatter finds its groove. K rekindles our flame; sparks spiral skyward like the sparks in my veins. With no preamble I retrieve Prince from the glove box, then forage through my gym bag to produce a blue plate wrapped in tissue paper. To K's horror I hold the toad with one hand and press my thumbs against various glands, squirting milky venom onto the dry plate. As it dries, it turns the color and texture of rubber cement. Minutes later I scrape the residue into the pipe I stole from the hippies.

I offer K a toke and am secretly pleased when he declines.

After an awkward silence, he says, "A toad named Prince, huh?"

"Just so you know," I say, "I was groomed to be a preacher. Sometimes it comes out when, you know, I'm seeing things."

"You ever turn violent?"

"Not yet. But feel free to kill me if I do."

"Sure thing, boss."

And so it begins. The smoky nectar burns in my mouth, my head, and my lungs before I feel it leaching into my bloodstream. I've only ever had one bad trip on this stuff and thankfully this doesn't feel like another one. The first wave turns the forest into a kaleidoscope of grays and greens. The second wave is jazz, snippets of Coltrane bopping through the second movement of *A Love Supreme*, my heart keeping time with the inimitable Elvin Jones. Then I can smell a mixture of Katie's skin and mom's spice rack. Diamonds wink in my peripheral vision and I have the sensation of sifting endless mounds of dry soil with my hands. A voice not unlike mine alternates between laughing and whimpering, sometimes both together. My bloodstream teems with warm chlorophyll, my legs take root in the soil and spider out in every direction, my arms multiply and sprout impossibly-hued leaves. My last cognizant impression is one of me towering over a wide-eyed semi-stranger with a sermon welling up inside me. I think the stranger's name begins with K.

MY RELATIONSHIP WITH MY FATHER devolved into a series of nods and grunts and public pleasantries. Somewhere along the way, he'd lost the ability to distinguish between the mission and the ministry. Arrogance and the almighty dollar blurred the lines between the sacred and tacitly profane. This became clear to me on my seventeenth birthday when he excused himself from my party to take a phone call in his office. Shoulders touching, Mom and I cut the cake and dished the ice cream for a gaggle of friends and aunts and cousins assembled to exaggerate yet another meaningless milestone. Ten minutes later I was dispatched to Dad's office to tell him his ice cream was melting. But as I raised my hand to knock I heard Katie's name. After a wave of guilt—I'd failed to pause even once that day to stop and think about my sister—I turned my ear and listened.

"I know, Stan. I know. But we can't keep borrowing money just to save a few employees. We either need a new bag of tricks or the layoffs are inevitable."

Stan Ewing was Dad's business manager and maybe the only decent human being in their waning religious empire. He was a whiz with numbers and knew more dirty jokes than the drummer in my band.

"Yeah, yeah, yeah," Dad said. "But as much as I hate to admit it, we've milked the whole Katie angle dry. It's got no traction any more."

He went silent for a few beats, then laughed.

"Unless you know any lepers we can heal or any more dead daughters to—"

The first blow missed the target. It caught Dad in the ear and sent the phone skittering across the hardwood. Between his shock and my momentum, his cordovan chair flipped backward and I was on top of him, showering fists into his miserable face. My tears mixed with his blood and skewed cartilage.

Mother found us sprawled on the office floor, Dad unconscious and me flailing impotently with my broken hand and weeping.

I don't remember, but mom swore I kept repeating, "You promised, Daddy. You promised Katie you'd get her all healed up."

I'M FLAT ON MY BACK, basking in the hallucinogenic afterglow when I smell coffee. The sky is a big blue bowl of popcorn clouds. A twin engine prop plane buzzes somewhere above and behind me. The best part of abusing Prince's venom is the sweet, velvety hangover—no nasty headaches or heartburn, just lapping waves of melancholy and a few twisted memories.

"You okay?" I recognize the voice, but still can't place anything but the K.

"Yeah," I say, my tongue pasted to the inside of my mouth. "So far so good."

"That was some show you put on last night. Kind of like fire-and-brimstone with a dapple of honey."

I respond by grinning and moaning.

"Tell me something, is the Repo Man supposed to be Jesus?"

"I guess so. I don't know, maybe."

He's quiet for a while, then says, "Thanks."

"For what?" I say, although I think I know the answer. I can see the change in his eyes. He's not my first convert. And frankly, if not for the lingering effects of toad venom, it would really piss me off.

"I can't explain it really," he says. "I guess you could say I found Jesus, or he found me or something. Either way, you introduced us and now I got my walking papers, so to speak. So, like I said, thanks."

"Great, my life's calling. I'm pimping for a God I have no use for." But that's not entirely true and I know it. Dad was right; my heart was hardened, but more like glass than iron. And behold, when the Repo Man stood at the door and knocked, he used a tire iron and shattered it into a million pieces. And as hard as I rail against it, I sense my own conversion metastasizing in bits and pieces, patched and pasted and quilted with only minimal and begrudging consent from me. But my inner cynic refuses to concede or admit anything. "Hate to break it to you partner, but you're about to trade the best years of your life for a few cheap religious thrills."

He's quiet again, then says, "Listen, just so you know, I took your toad down to the creek and let him go. I think he was killing you, man."

I stare at my shoes, resolved to press my rage through the fog in my brain. A twig snaps somewhere in the distance and I realize I'm alone. "Hey man, what's your name again?"

But he's already gone.

NOTHING CAN SEPARATE NANCY J. NORDENSON

THE CHURCH IS FULL. My husband and I find a seat by squeezing into the end of a hardwood pew that already holds its share of occupants. Along the back wall of the sanctuary stands a line of young men who, only days before, finished their junior year of high school. Several are missing a morning date with their number-two pencils and a standardized college aptitude exam. Their usual Saturday garb has been replaced with dress shirts, neckties, and for a few, a sportscoat or suit. They stand shoulder to shoulder in support of a young man who has not yet entered the sanctuary. My youngest son is among them.

The sanctuary is full of June sunlight streaming in from the stained glass skylights in the vaulted white ceiling and from the banks of clear windows wrapped around its sides like brackets, reflecting off the walls of white to blanket us as we wait for the service to begin. Sunlight in abundance is a gift received with relief and gratitude at the end of a long Minnesota winter. Light has overcome the darkness and we are safe from the shadows for another several months.

The pews in front of me are empty and we wait for those who would sit there to enter. The air smells of polished wood and air conditioning. I am a stranger to this church but to the side and behind me are familiar faces. Most of those that I recognize are parents or other family members of the young men lined up in the back. We usually greet each other on the soccer field sidelines or after a concert in the school auditorium, not on a Saturday morning in our Sunday best in a sanctuary awash with light.

I assume the unfamiliar faces are from other communities associated with the family for whom we are here. Close family and more distant relatives. I can see the familial DNA in that woman's coloring, that man's hair, the line of that boy's nose. Work colleagues and neighbors. Old roommates and church friends. Friends of his. Friends of hers. Friends of the kids.

A choir has been assembled. Some of the finest voices in the area, minus one tenor. The prelude begins with selections from Rachmaninoff's "Vespers." The choir sings in Russian but the words printed in the bulletin are English.

Dnes' spasenie miru byst' poem voskresshemu iz groba i nachal'niku zhizni nasheya…Today, salvation has come to the world. Let us sing to Him who rose from the dead, the Author of our life. Having destroyed death by death, He has given us the victory and great mercy… Thou didst rise from the tomb and burst the bonds of Hades! Thou didst destroy the condemnation of death…

As the choir shifts in tone, Orthodox majesty is traded for a clear and simple Shaker hymn arranged by William Hawley:

*Not one sparrow is forgotten,
E'en the raven God will feed;
And the lily of the valley
From His bounty hath its need.*

The choir is no longer singing in a language we can't understand. As the syllables merge, the multilingual transcontinental meaning that began in Russian and ended in Americana pierces us. We're reminded why we're here.

A father of four. Young. Handsome, talented and strong. Dead at his own hand. I'm not sure who in the room knows this piece of the story. Family wishes no doubt have left some wondering how a man in his prime can die for a cause unknown although the puzzle can't be left long without this dark piece falling into place.

Only days before, I walked up the basement stairs to see a good friend standing in my front doorway, eyes swollen, dressed in black. She whispered the news, mouthed it really. The web of notifications, phone calls, offers of assistance had begun. The activity that would culminate in this Saturday morning had been set in motion. Communities anchored in schools and soccer teams and church congregations and family circles were now coalescing around a single defining piece of news.

The choir finishes and the door to the sanctuary opens. The shepherd priest leads the father of four, his sons and daughters, the mother of his children, and his own mother and father and brothers and sisters to a place in the back of the church. They stop at the pool of water. What they are doing there is a mystery to me. The Protestant funerals of my heritage begin with the coffin at the front of the church and there is no mystery taking place in the back. The priest speaks but the mystery holds my focus more than the words. The oldest daughter sprinkles holy water on the coffin, perhaps hoping it will penetrate the steel vault and revive her father like a splash of water to the face. I know there is a deeper theological meaning to the sprinkle, but hoping for magic to be added to mystery is perhaps the deepest theology. The pall is spread and the family proceeds to take their places in the reserved pews, leaving the occupied coffin in the front position of honor.

With everyone now in place, we stand to sing. The words and music are in the bulletin. Only the melody line is printed and so we all sing the same notes. If this had been a Protestant funeral, the bass, tenor, alto, and soprano voices would have divided. Melody only is pure community. Father, let them be one. We are one in the key of F# minor.

"GREAT GOD OF MERCY, *God of consolation*," we sing. "*Look on your people, gathered here to praise you: Pity our weakness, come in pow'r to aid us, Source of all blessing.*"

Who were we, this group of more than nine hundred gathered in corporate grief and love, we who were asking the great God of mercy and consolation to look on us?

We grieved for the death of this man, mourned the gap of his presence in our community, anticipated and wished we could remove the pain that his family, particularly his children, would carry forward with them for a lifetime. But was the weakness of this grief all for which we begged pity? Did we—God's people—need his power only to assist with our mourning? Were we fine but for this moment?

"JESUS REDEEMER, Lord of all creation," we sing. "Come as our Savior, Jesus, friend of sinners: Grant us forgiveness, lift our downcast spirit, heal us and save us."

Together we claim to be sinners standing on the floor below the priest together with the man for whom we grieve. Be our friend, Jesus, in spite of it. Banded together with downcast spirits, acute and chronic, we reel inside, scream, weep against the choice one of our own has made. Do we weep for more? It is the very ubiquitousness of downcast spirits that pricks me.

Ask me what I know of suicide and I will have to admit, very little. In contrast, ask me what I know of a downcast spirit, of despair, and I will answer that it has indeed visited me from time to time.

We're all despair's spokesperson. We've each flirted with hopelessness, imagined ourselves to be the forgotten sparrow. We've each lost our innocence. There are things we must admit and they are terrifying: that life is fragile, that well-executed work may fail, that financial security isn't secure, that relationships can become broken so badly that the pieces no longer match, that we can lose track of the meaning we thought our life once had, that despite all our best efforts, the course of life may be shifted in a second into dangerous, scary, heart-wrenching territory. To experience any one of these realizations is to shake hands and look eye-to-eye with despair. Even in the briefest encounter, one never forgets its face.

Despair and I locked eyes one night in 1988. The setting: An emergency room. The reason for the meeting: My oldest son, four years old, had fallen from a ladder onto a cement floor, hitting his head. His brain was filled with blood. Pupils fixed and dilated. Reflexes absent. Bleak, everything was so bleak. Hush fell around us when we passed. Eyes of sympathy upon us. We were the parents no one wanted to be. While we were shifted to a private waiting room and introduced to Father Roger, a chaplain who was assigned to look after only us, my unconscious unresponsive little boy was intubated and connected to a respirator. My youngest son, then fifteen months, was toddling around barefoot—no time to grab shoes—oblivious to the fact that he was on the threshold of losing his brother, of becoming an only child.

There was hope, some hope, by operating on his brain, the neurosurgeon said with his words. Hope wasn't offered in his eyes, however, in his spirit, or in the air around us. Surgery would release the pressure of the hemorrhage. Spare the brain some damage. No promises. The description of the surgery was cut short when a nurse opened the door and summoned the doctor to quickly return to his patient. The possibility of hope that had entered the room with the doctor also left the room with him. Imagining our son coding, my husband and I knew there would be no need for surgery.

My eyes water and throat tightens with the recollection. All our moments of despair remain in us like a song we learned as children that only requires a few notes to pull up and take over our mental space, playing over and over again as if it had never stopped. We don't want to revisit the meeting with despair, be reminded of the story, be reminded that bad things happen. We fear the aphorism is wrong and that indeed lightening will strike twice. We want nothing to do with passing through the waters, passing through the river, walking through the fire despite the great God of mercy's promise that we will not be alone, swept over, or set ablaze. The recollection of despair is enough to invite despair's face back into the room.

How great was this man's despair?, I wonder.

"JOY-GIVING SPIRIT, *be our light in darkness,*" we sing. "*Come to befriend us, help us bear our burdens: Give us true courage, breathe your peace around us, Stay with us always.*"

Help us bear our burdens, Spirit. We ask. We plead. Burden bearing is easier when shared. To be alone is to have no one to help pull your hand away from that of despair, to have no one to help break the stare.

But for Father Roger, we were alone in our waiting room. We were seventy miles from home. Although my sister and brother-in-law were on their way as soon as they heard the news, there was no one to call who could say, "I'll be there in five minutes." The telephone became the instrument of the Spirit, the conduit by which our burden was shared with the living communion of saints. We called parents who were across the country and a couple friends and asked them to pray, asked them to ask others to pray. We didn't need anything from them but their tether of love to us and a share of their tether to God's love. Despair tethered by love makes it bearable.

The question begs to be asked, how did we who are sitting here now in sorrow tether love to this man in an act of burden bearing before the events of this past week unfolded? Was the line-up of prayer from this community around this man and his family as strong several formative months ago as the line-up of young men in the back of the room is today?

"GOD IN THREE PERSONS, *Trinity eternal,*" we sing. "*Come to renew us, fill your Church with glory: Grant us your healing, pledge of resurrection, Foretaste of heaven.*"

Grant us your healing, Father, Son, and Spirit. Grant this crowd your healing. This family, your healing. My son, your healing.

A miracle. That's the word more than one doctor used. There was no explanation for why one moment, my son was going to die or live in a nearly dead state, and the next moment, was going to be fine. When the surgeon had left us alone in our private waiting room to catch a vision of life without our son he entered a room in which my son was semi-conscious, sitting up, and trying to remove his intravenous line and other cords and tubes. We had been brought to the screaming edge of a great cliff and in a flash the space in front of us became level. To our prayers, our pleading, God had responded by drying the intracerebral hemorrhage. Like the red sea the blood was held back making way for life. Healing; resurrection; foretaste of heaven.

The recollection isn't over, however. The arc is not yet complete.

* * *

WE SING THE LAST NOTE. The mourners take their seats.

Friends come forward and share their reminiscences. Scripture is read. Great is thy faithfulness, the great lament reminds us. We are led beside still water, so says the Psalmist.

A well-dressed man stands, steps out from the congregation, and walks up the steps to the lectern. I don't know who he is but he has the face of a respected grandfather with graying hair and confident posture. His reading assignment is from the eighth chapter of Romans. He doesn't read it, however. He speaks it. He appears to have it memorized—hidden in his heart—and it flows out from that deep place.

Head held high he asks the question, "Who will separate us from the love of Christ?"

His face moves slowly across the crowd. "Will hardship, or distress, or persecution, or famine, or nakedness, or peril, or sword?"

His eyes gently meet ours. "No, in all these things we are more than conquerors through Him who loved us."

Slowly and intently he proceeds. "For I am convinced that neither death, nor life, nor angels, nor rulers, nor things present, nor things to come, nor powers, nor height, nor depth, nor anything else in all creation, will be able to separate us from the love of God in Christ Jesus our Lord."

By the time he finishes, I'm sure he has met every eye before him with deliberate care.

The priest adds the word of Jesus; blessed are the poor in spirit; blessed are those who mourn. In those eleven words we are all included.

The priest takes his place and begins the hardest sort of homily I can imagine. Even so, he appears willing to give guidance and comfort to this crowd and so I take out my red notebook and pen.

"THERE ARE TRUTHS WE NEED TO KNOW," the priest says, "*that will help us face death squarely and truly.*"

Yes, please, Father. My pen waits to record these truths. What are we missing? What is the missing X that will help us figure out Y? Y being the mystery of life that holds death and perplexity and despair.

"THE WORLD IS NOT AS IT SEEMS," the priest continues. "*When the cord of life is cut our soul begins its true journey, sees the vision it has groped for its whole life.*"

Groped is a good word. To reach about uncertainly, to feel one's way. The Psalms are full of disorientation. Directed travel gone awry. Being hit in the face by despair. By the rivers of Babylon we sit and weep with the thought of Zion, the "something more" that keeps us searching, the unrest until we find our rest in thee.

When the groping is over, the priest tells us that "we will stand in the light of all that is true." It is this moment, he says, that is "the glory of our faith."

"That all-seeing eye, the one who is judge is the one who died for us," he tells us. Knowing his audience, the priest adds, "The judge is the defense attorney." Without looking around, I sense the bond the priest has just made with many sitting before him.

"CHRIST KNOWS WE WILL BE TEMPTED *to perplexity and despair,*" the priest says. "*It is part of being a fallen race. Christ is not perplexed, however, and He is with us.*"

The priest reminds us that Christ was at the

grave of Lazarus, dead three days, his sisters weeping, accusing him of being absent while they were in despair and their brother was dying. He could have saved them all from this fate.

My mind brings up the image it always does when hearing the Lazarus story, not of a mummy-like figure stumbling out of the grave but of a weeping man stumbling toward the grave. Overcome with emotion, overcome with grief, the weeping man stopped at least twice. It is impossible to walk while weeping without becoming disoriented. Why was he weeping? Didn't he know he was going to end the grief in just a few minutes by bringing Lazarus back into being? Or did the human wallop of despair disorient even Christ, blinding him to the great glory of our faith that is at the end of our groping?

"I am the resurrection and the life. Do you believe?" asked the weeping man-God, apparently not thinking that the weeping compromised the vision for which the souls of Mary and Martha groped, the vision they associated with his presence: healing; resurrection; foretaste of heaven. Weeping and authority, despair and belief, grief and life coexisting in Christ.

But Lazarus did emerge and the weeping stopped.

"HE IS A MAGICIAN," the priest says. "*He can bring life from death, light from dark, joy from sadness.*"

With my son stable, the neurosurgeon sent him via ambulance to the Life Support Unit at the children's hospital in the city where we lived for further tests and surveillance. By now it was nearing midnight. I rode in the ambulance the seventy miles, with my husband and younger son following behind in our car. The paramedic and my son were in the back well of the ambulance. I sat in the front passenger seat shivering from nerves, turning my head once for every couple miles to ask, "How's he doing?"

Arrangements had been made between the hospitals and so a neurosurgeon and a bed were waiting for him when we arrived. "Do you know who I am?" I asked as I came alongside his gurney. Yes, he knew. Despair, whose grip had already begun to loosen, was now released. Pupil check, normal. Reflex check, normal. New CAT scan, normal. The massive brain hemorrhage of hours before was evidenced now only by the mark of a single drop of blood on otherwise healthy gray matter. All was well. The new neurosurgeon shrugged his shoulders in unknowing.

NOTHING CAN SEPARATE US FROM HIS LOVE, the priest echoes.

Ah, so it was because of God's great love for my son that he said let there be absolution of cerebral bleeding, let there be restoration of reflexes, let there be movement of pupils, let there be not even a headache to scar this precious child. For God so loved my son that he... But the logic of "If A, then B" fails here.

"Can I have another root beer popsicle?" my son responded when the nurse asked if he wanted another frozen treat.

The nurse looked around the open unit, motioning with her head for him to also look. He was the only child awake, the only one not in a coma. He was her only popsicle customer.

"Of course you can," she said. "No one else is eating them."

The parents of the children in the other beds would have liked to have gathered up the root beer, the banana, and the orange quiescently frozen confections and provided a feast to their children if they would only awaken. For God did not love their son, their daughter?, they wondered as they groped home, popsicles uneaten, unrequested.

Back to before the relief of healing, back to the cave of the waiting room to recall the still small voice that preceded the resorbed bleeding and popsicles. God is not in the wind, the earthquake, the fire and God's love is not in the dramatic recovery. In that waiting room I had thought of some friends whose daughter had been born shortly before my son. Severe anomalies. Whether she would live was questionable. Whether she would be "normal" was not as questionable. I remembered them telling us that as they sat beside her in neonatal intensive care waiting for a sign that the shift toward life had occurred, that they had prayed for her to belong to God. As I remembered this, I prayed it also for my son with his pupils fixed. I knew I had to pray this. The prayer of Gethsemane. Tears streaming. Take this cup away. Nonetheless, your will not mine. God, let him be yours.

The priest called Him a magician. Annie Dillard calls Him a maniac. "There is not a guarantee in the world," she writes. Sure, our needs are met. The warranty of ask; seek; knock never fails to secure the needs of an imploring spirit. In spite of this covenant, it is impossible not to notice that creatures and people die. "And one day it occurs to you that you must not need life. Obviously. And then you're gone. You have finally understood that you're dealing with a maniac."

WITH MY PRAYER CAME AN IMAGE. There was a cupped hand. Inside the hand was my son. This hand that cradled my son started out level and on the ground, then moved up but remained level. No matter the position of the hand—up or down—it made no difference to the safekeeping of my son. Whether here or removed from here my son was in the same place, cradled in God's hand: needs met, living or dying.

I bow my head in unknowing.

JESUS SAID NOTHING can snatch his own out of the Father's hand. Can we roll out? Crawl out? Take a misstep in our groping and become lost? Can we become so disoriented that we don't recognize our status in the hand? Does despair cause us to thrash about so that we feel that indeed we have been either snatched or let go? Does despair cause us to lodge ourselves between his fingers burrowing so far into the crack that we feel as if we are about to fall a fall that will never end? Does God then roll his hand over—like a magic trick in which the hand is faster than the eye—to catch us or pinch us at the nape of the neck? Does he hang on to us by the hairs on our heads, as we dangle and try to break free of his fingers?

Hush now, says the community to the one thrashing about in the hand. Be at peace. The communion of saints joins Julian of Norwich in reorienting the disoriented, "All shall be well and all shall be well and all manner of things shall be well." All the while, the community is murmuring in audible or inaudible voices to God: hang on to this child of yours; keep your hand cupped.

The prayers of the community align with those of Christ. None of us want to be forgotten, to be separated from the hand, from the love. We don't want it for ourselves; we don't want it for those we love. As a meal is shared, the thrasher is nudged back toward center. As an hour is spent talking, the despairer unburrows from the crack between the fingers.

I'm trying to remember, did I pray for this man

last month, last year? Or did I pray only for my friend, his ex-wife? It shames me that I can't remember. What thrashing about did my lack of prayer not restrain? Father, forgive me for I have sinned.

The Liturgy of the Eucharist begins. More words. More music. Streams of people go forward to eat Christ's body, drink Christ's blood. I want to join them, my friends. We have the same tears in our eyes, the same hunger and thirst for divine peace. More mystery.

THE BULLETIN INCLUDES THE WORDS,
"In its final act, the Christian community gives G~ over, body and soul, to the fullness of God's heavenly kingdom."

God's hand still cradles. Whatever thrashing about despair had triggered in this man has ceased. We, the Christian community, now let go. By grace we're invited to participate in this final act. Whatever we did or didn't do at the soccer sidelines, the school auditorium, the work office space, the neighborhood sidewalk, the church narthex, the kitchen table, or the prayer closet is passed. The cupped hand moves up to the full presence of the weeping God-man who has already died for the man he now sees face to face.

The glory of our faith.

THE CHOIR RISES TO SING, this time the Latin of Faure's "Requiem",

In Paradisum deducant te Angeli in tuo adventu….. May angels lead you into Paradise; At your coming may martyrs receive you, and may they lead you into the Holy City, Jerusalem, May the chorus of angels receive you, And with Lazarus, who once was a pauper, may you have eternal rest.

The priest offers a final blessing and invites us to sing. Once again, we transition from music that floats down from above in a tongue we don't speak to music that licks the ground and rises up from within us. This time the parts are separated out and I relax as the bass, the alto, the tenor are restored.

I heard the voice of Jesus say, "I am this dark world's light; Look unto me, thy morn shall rise, And all thy day be bright." I looked to Jesus, and I found in him my Star, my Sun; And in that light of life I'll walk till trav'ling days are done.

The young men in the back file out. We turn and empty the pew. Much of the afternoon is still ahead. Time enough for a nap under the late-spring sun. Time enough for coffee at a sidewalk table. The shadow of winter will no doubt return; but for now, we've been given light.

Text of "Great God of Mercy" by James Quinn, S.J. from Resource Collection of Hymns and Service Music for the Liturgy
© 1981, International Committee on English in the Liturgy, Inc. (ICEL). All rights reserved.

SUNDAY SCHOOL LESSON JILL BERGKAMP

It was her talk of escape
that caught the boys' attention,
flattening a Joshua made of felt
as she lowered him
from the woman's window.

They sang, "Rahab saved her family,"
to the tune of London Bridges,
then ate some graham crackers
with grape juice.

Their teacher passed out scissors,
and asked them to cut their own
scenes of walls with men clambering down.
Ribbons were passed, and tugged
through the hands of the harlot.

The boys were bungee jumping Joshua,
"Ka-plum," from the bricked barrier,
Parachute-straps were fashioned,
then slings,
and the girls

savoring their dark juice,
thought of how it might feel,
being somebody's Savior,
of holding the line of that rope
in the night.

ADVENT KRISTIN MULHERN NOBLIN

This year, we broke things.
I stood on the pavement, watched
bottle
        bottle
                bottle
                        shatter.

Some days, but not all days,
I wonder how many people
enjoy the glitzy lights,
how many people lose Jesus
somewhere in the waiting.

      *

Last summer,
Robert looked at me,
asked how I
in my private college
white skin
rich family
suburban-cushioned life
could possibly understand
what it was like
to lose everything,
to have people walk by
pretending to read
The Wall Street Journal,
to be so drugged up
cast out
written off,

the gum people pull off their shoes—
how could I know
what it was to need,
to breathe, Jesus
with my last breath?

Maybe I am weaker.
Maybe it takes less to get my attention.
Maybe this isn't a contest I want to win.
Silenced, I pulled myself off
the bottom of his shoe,
walked back into my life
of air-conditioned cars
and ten pairs of shoes,
not understanding anything.

    *

When does it happen?
When does pain
stop discriminating
and all pain
become one pain—
that pain
on that hill,
that Friday?

    *

The glass shards glistened
on the rain-soaked cement.
And it is there,
picking through the fragments,
that I find him
lying in a manger
of silence—
pauses between forced excitement,
unspoken blame,

ADVENT

walls with holes that echo
some other argument
some other time.

Come, oh come—
God with us in the bleached walls of the shelter,
the four Christmas dinners,
the project homes where kids
wear their only socks
until they're black with dirt.
God with us, the baby,
arms folded tightly across his body,
offering the promise—
something new out of broken glass.

    *

We broke bottles this Christmas.
One for me.
One for Robert.
One for everyone who's met
loss on that barren road,
grimaced, and walked on.

SILENCE KRISTIN MULHERN NOBLIN

Because I ask for silence
Don't think I am going to die;
It is just the opposite with me.
    —Pablo Neruda

When I reached for her,
I had no words, no plan
to console the girl sobbing on the floor,
hidden between the rows of chairs.
This is not what I do—
I have left the counseling to others.

For half an hour,
I pressed my hand on her back,
leaned my forehead on the chair in front of me,
willed peace into her body
while everything her mom and dad were not
pooled on the carpet beneath her.
And her tears were mine—
adolescent and lying on the floor,
unable to love two people
who no longer loved each other
yet pulled too tight between them to escape.
We were two women:
both the war-tugged rope
and the sought-after prize
broken in this struggle,
broken and unable to ask,
How long will this continue?
How many times must this story recur,
before we taste redemption?

Climbing onto the chair beside me,
she leaned into my arm.
She looked to me for hope
more sturdy than a feather;
I could offer no more
than a road and a promise
I only sometimes believed.

BREATH OF WATER CHUCK BAKER

I'm a famine in the land,
a deep well, filled with earth,
seed wasted and scattered
among thorns and thistles.

Even my tongue
is thick with sand,
in search of water,
a buried breath.

My brother's blood—
First Sign
of a crying, creeping sea—
Dark Water,
A Serpent in the way.

Then Starlight sears
the frost by night,
and sunrise fire—
the sun, the moon, and eleven stars—
bring the dew of heaven.

It pools on my flesh,
sucks into my bones—
Hot springs in the wilderness—
A morning vision
of deep waters within

It is enough.

THE THROAT CHUCK BAKER

The throat

is an open grave.

Words, cords of death,
Ensnare, tighten,
Like a serpent's grip—
Battling breath,
Cutting flesh
Like sharp   s   words—
Drawn first to protect,

Then to kill.

The blood that slithers
Out is a snake's venom
From a forked tongue—
Poisoned poetry
That seeks to cover
Its mistakes, bury
Them alive,

Until all that remains
is a cold reminder
of a warmth
that was.

MOURNING PEGGY SMITH DUKE

The Church Street preacher
nodded, sighed, lightly perched
on the crowded grief-worn couch.
He clutched Jesus in his hand,
patted her knee, and said,
"Mrs. T, we pray the Lord
will be with you." He rose, smiled,
backed through the front door
eyeing the empty rented bed still
sitting in the center of the room.

The Main Street preacher
greeted, laughed, never stopped
until he reached the kitchen.
He sat down at the table,
took a cup of coffee and said
"Miz T, what do you need done?"
He scooped up her car keys,
snapped the screen on the back door
and headed for the Goodyear store
for four new tires.

MORE THAN THE BURN BRITTANY HAMPTON

"The poor and needy search for water, but there is none; their tongues are parched with thirst. But I the LORD will answer them; I, the God of Israel, will not forsake them."
    —Isaiah 41:17

She is thirsty
the little girl with a navy dress.
Her hair is knotted. She scratches at it
sometimes violently, sometimes habitually.
Turn on the faucet, water will come.
One drop, then two, then brown
splashing in the sink, spitting filth into her cupped hands.
She drinks.

Dirty face. Saltines, two in a pack
brought home from school. Mother will be home soon
to tuck the girl in, into the bed with a sleeping bag
and three blankets. It will be cold still.
Socks, gloves, a towel wrapped around her feet.
It will be cold still.

Her teacher says she needs a bath. Sends a note home.
So now she stands in front of the tub, turns the knob.
Not even brown water comes. So her hair will itch, her face will smudge,
her skin will smell, and her teacher
will take notice.

Mother is home. Circles under her eyes like dark moons.
A girl in a navy dress jumps into her arms. Smiles come.
They hug to feel something more
than the burn in their stomachs.

STRICTER JUDGEMENT HEATHER VON DOEHREN

Working the Sunday double-shift
at least her mother babysat for free.

While the midmorning sun crisscrossed shadows
against the altar of scrambled eggs and juice carafes

formal attire elevated
in opposite proportion to the tips.

She needed to pay rent this week.
She needed a miracle.

Pouring decaf into eight mugs, listening to change
clink in her pocket, little by little, growing

she received her tip:
a bible tract speaking simple words of encouragement.

Fucking Christians, she thought while
enduring such afflictions

silently awaiting
her second break.

ON CHILDREN, SEWERS, AND DICTATORS KIMBERLY GEORGE

Ema lies in the corner, slamming her head to dusty pavement. Her little body convulses with the violence.

Across the courtyard, I hold in each arm twin babies found last week on the front porch, delivered like the morning bread. Their tiny bodies fight their mother's glue addiction in struggled, wheezing breaths. I feed them warm, noontime bottles while Lina, my favorite five-year-old, surrenders to tears. Having just returned from "visiting" her mother, she cries out in pain as her mother drives away. Not the pain of the black eye, acquired after not meeting her midnight quota, but the pain of separation. Lina's mom uses her to beg at night on the streets of Bucharest and returns her exhausted. As I feed the babies, she wants to climb up to be held, jealous of the new ones occupying my arms. I set the babies down and scoop her up, noticing her little head is covered with fleas. Her tears crescendo to a wail. I hold her closer and resolve to get Lina (and now myself) a dose of flea shampoo.

Overwhelmed, and not sure how to triage the needs, I watch Ema's tantrum grow more acute. Serban rushes to the corner, kneeling down to rescue her from herself. She resists, flailing with uncanny strength for a two-year-old body. Her tiny frame seems to harbor rage, caged within and warring off every offer of touch. Ema challenges the vitality of my faith, more so than any child here. Lina, though harmed and hurting, receives nurturing with a child's embrace. The tiny lungs of the twins will one day heal. Yet for Ema, I retreat to a hopeless ache. Of the small staff of workers, only Serban can nurture her. His hands hold her as she fights, until, exhausted, she trusts his arms to fall asleep in.

I watch Serban with a certain awe, remembering what I had heard of his life before the Romanian orphanage. Nearby Moldavia is his home country. There he trained in an elite unit of the army and, at twenty-two, had achieved a position of prominence in a country suffering with poverty. Yet, he had recently left it behind and come here, to a chaotic home outside of Bucharest. Hands skilled in war now hold the fatherless. I was told that in leaving the army and arriving here, Serban had gone through a deeply spiritual experience. I wanted to hear his story, to understand the young man who chose such an unconventional exchange. But I would never know the words of his story: Serban does not speak English, and I do not know any of the four languages in which he is fluent. Thus, our friendship develops in tacit communication.

Serban made his life in this place. I am attempting a lone summer while on break from college classes. A solo journey from Seattle to Bucharest brought me here, and from the moment I first stood on the front porch, jet-lagged and wary, nothing was as I had supposed. Memory paints the indelible image when teenage girls blared Romanian techno on the front porch while rocking themselves incessantly, as newborn babies. Hugging themselves and rocking, I would discover, is how many of the orphans pass their days. They are sixteen and seventeen, some with babies of there own, yet seem locked in their own perpetual, tormented childhood. This home is a refuge for orphans and street children of every kind: newborns to teens to young twenty-somethings, all marginalized by a society still suffering the effects of a former regime.

I meet Uta the day of my arrival and she takes my hand to tour the dusty roads of her village. Uta is fifteen and seven months pregnant, with a feisty, sweet spirit. We walk the roads and she points out the landmarks: a convenience store on the corner, an alcohol factory down the street. "Bad men," she explains, pointing to the dilapidated building. As we walk, two teenage boys realize there is a new girl in town and begin pelting me with rocks. Luckily, they never would have made the baseball team and the rocks fall an arm's length away. Uta proves a pugnacious heroine and tries to run after them, but I convince her to let them go. We arrive back at the home and she wants to make me lunch. Meticulously she cuts up garden vegetables, a precious commodity. She has prepared a bowl brimming with cucumbers and tomatoes when one of the boys starts teasing her. Her spirit blazes and soon the bowl of tomatoes is a projectile. The victim is covered with tomato muck, and so is my sleeping cot, which happens to be in the line of fire. She grins sheepishly at me and begins helping me pick up the pieces. With no extra sheets and little time to wash them, I find tomatoes in my bed for weeks later.

The immediate needs of the orphanage provide no break for orientation. Feeding sixty mouths, changing diapers, breaking up fights... the days carry a rhythm of chaos. But in the long, hot nights in Romania, the day's momentum collides with a frightening calm. The incessant flies, fleas, and moaning of the stray dogs will not let my tired mind sleep. From my window I see the outline of the alcohol factory down the street. I watch the moon cast shaded light on my pillow while my thoughts revisit the day's moments. I need the stillness of the night to process, to feel my own response, to allow my own sorrow, to encounter this darkness.

Six-thirty comes early. Sunflower fields, just outside my window, greet the horizon's burnished light. The bread man travels up our dusty walk, and I scurry to meet him. Thirty loaves of fresh bread delivered every morning! Romania has its joys. I pay the deliveryman and begin buttering bread in preparation for the frenzy of breakfast. The weight of last night's sleeplessness lightens with the fresh morning. The house is still asleep, and I revel in the rare quiet. Too soon my moment comes and goes. At first only small stirrings, then the unleashing of the morning's commotion: fists banging on the door of our only bathroom, hungry mouths scrambling to the kitchen for bread, and the blare of the incessant radio. A lover of quiet, I cannot understand the compulsion for constant noise which seems to consume the space of thought.

Perhaps not thinking is the escape route of the long suffering. It is a survival skill. The daily pain these children experience challenges the imagination, as most have known every form of abuse. The older ones grew up state-run institutions. During those bleak years, Romania's dictator Nicolae Ceausescu was committed to amassing his population even in the midst of widespread poverty. Many families could no longer care for their children and gave them up to state care. In 1989, when Ceausescu was deposed and the orphan crisis became exposed, it was estimated 150,000 orphans were living in state sponsored facilities—many in horrific conditions of abuse and malnourishment. Perhaps worst of all was the severe neglect: babies growing up without eye contact, touch, or bonding. The neglect will manifest itself in a myriad of ways, often in forms of self-stimulation. It is shocking to see the orphans poking their own eyes or habitually rocking themselves. But my shock soon subsides, as I get accustomed to the familiar.

Cleaning up breakfast, I gaze out the kitchen window and fight weary despair. The older girls spend their morning rocking to their radio. Ema is throwing another fit, Lina cries for her mother, and I mechanically go about my tasks. I enlist Lina's help. She is delighted to be chosen for the job and soon is distracted from thinking of her mother. Lina's mother, like many of the parents of the little ones here, lives on the streets. She is an orphan herself, and having no resources, leaves her child with us to be housed and fed. And since she still holds legal rights to her daughter, she comes to take her away periodically depending on her pocketbook. Lina's nighttime begging supports her mother's glue addiction, the drug of choice on Bucharest streets. While ruining brain and lung cells, it offers fleeting relief from hunger pains.

Lina's five year old laugher invites me back to our present. Serban has just announced an afternoon excursion—a field trip to the nearby river. I hear the lovely stirring of childish pandemonium.

Mala and Tasha, fellow workers from Sri Lanka and Atlanta, help me pack sandwiches. Serban nicknames his friends "chocolate" and "vanilla," sheepishly trying out his two new English words. My laugher surprises me. I am still learning how to laugh in Romania.

Serban carts the kids in van-fulls down the dusty road, with the zealous speed of all his Romanian counterparts. I'm sure the oncoming traffic is headed right for us on these makeshift streets. But no one but me seems to notice because today is the day for our picnic at the river. Mirth prevails. It is a murky river and a polluted park, but it does not matter in the least to these kids. Sunshine and water are therapeutic. The fighting ceases for the afternoon. Splashing and laughter ensue. Every child, from two to twenty, remembers how to play. It is an unceasing chorus of "Watch me, watch me!" as they swim and and splash. There is joy here in Romania. The pain just threatens to drown it. Uta splashes with the rest, Lina runs around like a little monkey, and even Ema lounges in the sunshine, quiet and content with her world for an afternoon.

I almost, but not quite, let myself forget what had once, twice, probably many times occurred at this river. Two teenage girls, now under our care, had been camping on its shore. The "police" arrived to intimidate and arrest, but it happened that one of our workers was distributing food that night to the many kids living in the area. Fortunately the "police" were easily intimidated themselves and moved elsewhere with their solicitations. It is not uncommon knowledge in Romania that many teenage girls, orphaned and unprotected, are coerced into lives of sexual slavery. The numbers are rapidly escalating; the ages are drastically decreasing. And the economy is thriving on it. This river, once the laughter dies and the darkness comes, will again become a recruiting ground.

The river and church are the weekly field trips. On Sundays, Serban packs the kids into the van again and takes them to the nearby gypsy village for church. Cardboard and plastic are the building materials for small homes throughout the town. Much of the economy is sustained from brick making; sunshine and mud and many working hands. While most of the villagers struggle for an income to merely survive, their hospitality and joyful spirits exceeds that of my wealthiest American neighbors. We slide into pews in a one-room building. The singing and preaching is almost four hours long. Many of our girls grow uncomfortable and wiggle off the pews, talking loudly to one another. I am embarrassed by their distracting behavior. The preacher speaks passionately and smiles at his unruly guests. I reprimand the girls, but he acts unaware of their rudeness. Afterwards, he thanks us for coming and reminds me our girls are always welcome in his church. It is a rare, striking moment of acceptance.

***

ONE WEEKEND, the director of the orphanage wants Serban and me to take a trip up into the mountains to visit a sister-camp run for street kids. I look forward to it as a respite. Serban and I take the train up into the Carpathian mountains, to a tiny village once known for its resistance to Ceausescu. For its rebellious spirit under the Communist dictator, it was rewarded. Ceausescu had systematically exiled criminals and alcoholics to its city limits. Two decades later, the town is in economic ruin. The first night, we stay in town with the camp leaders. Our neighbor in the building, a seven-year-old girl, knocks on our door at 3:00 in the morning. Her older brother is beating up her father. She is scared he might kill him. We hear the bellowing of two intoxicated men.

The following morning, we take the gondola up to the base of the camp. I meet the camp leaders—many American volunteers—and tour their facilities. It's a wilderness camp, supported by people abroad and designed to teach the kids teamwork, self-confidence, and life skills. I split off from the group and hike up the mountain. At the top, I find an old church. I enter it, hear the creaking of its rusted door, and enter its pews to kneel. Aged icons line the walls. I've been reading Orthodox writers while here in Romania, and my experience seems to resonate with a common teaching: before we know faith, we must first wrestle authentically with uncertainty. Before we can speak of light, we must honestly engage the darkness. I hear the knocking of the little girl, hear her feet run for refuge in our flea-ridden apartment. I hear the screams of little Ema, throwing her body on the pavement. I think of Uta's nearing due date, and wonder what will become of a little, unborn child and her young mother. I ask God what hope looks like—here in Romania, kneeling on an old church floor.

AFTER SERBAN AND I RETURN from the mountain, it is just a week before I leave Romania. I had come with compassion and naiveté; I would leave humbled and searching. Before I say goodbye, Serban wants me to visit Bucharest at night, to see where our kids would be if not with us. The children on the streets make their home in the available sewers. I hesitate to go, sensing my own limit for exposure to pain has been met and surpassed. I have heard stories of the raw violence of Bucharest nightlife. The orphanage even keeps a photo journal to document some of the images. Yet, the album is not filled with the violence of the street kids, but shows the brutality of the police. It holds pages of burned teenagers, the result of the police lighting the sewers on fire with gasoline.

THAT NIGHT I GO WITH SERBAN and other workers into the city. Descending a ladder, we climb down into the darkness underground. It is always warm in the sewers and oppressively dark and claustrophobic, but to these teenagers it is home, and I want to respect that. They show me their makeshift living room and kitchen, proud of their place and community. I am told this is the Hilton of the sewers, relatively clean and safe. Hilton or not, I cannot believe people live like this.

Visiting the sewers has a dynamic I hardly expect. I want it to feel authentic, but it seems set up for a tourist business. Like visiting a museum, I donate my Romanian lei. The "tourist guide" is personable and gregarious, well versed in his lines. Crafted stories create just the right effect for larger contributions. The girls are excellent actresses, become your best friend, and recite fabricated stories designed to gain another dollar. False relationships, manipulated stories—there is creativity and skill in this livelihood they have found. I am drawn into the pathos, while feeling a strong sense of my own resistance. I don't want to be made a tourist to suffering.

Midway through the tour, I decide to come up for fresh air. I slowly climb the cold, metal ladder, pausing to view Ceausescu's palace haunting the horizon. Standing on the dank sewer steps, my head just emerged from underground; I view its grotesque glare and sense the omnipresence of history.

At one time, the dictator had housed his regime in one of Europe's grandest palaces, and these children, the product of his mad policies, now live in the sewers. These teenagers are the babies of the regime, raised in state institutions and then shunted to the streets to survive. Kids like Ema and Lina are thus the babies of the babies. In a dark cycle of abuse and poverty, I have no answers for hope. Gazing at the glare of the palace, my thoughts wander again to Lina's hurt, to Ema's self-inflicted violence. My body is weak with dizziness.

Five feet from the sewer, a fight breaks out. A man lies bleeding on the ground, the foot of a drunken, raging man slamming his face to the pavement. Night goers walk in and out of the nearby McDonald's. The beating continues, then casually halts.

I wait for Serban to emerge from underground. He ascends only in time to see the drunken man stumble away under the lamplight.

He walks me back to the car and extends his arm for comfort and protection. Physically ill, emotionally poisoned, I submit to my despair and try to convince Serban to do likewise. He quietly refuses, and in broken English, asks me if I know who the man is, the one drunken and raging.

"That's Dumitru, Ema's father," Serban explains. It seems the little girl's violence had not always been self-inflicted. Stunned, I see why it is that a child would need to learn to be held—why love could feel so frightening. And for a moment, grace becomes present and mysterious. I am reminded that what we do matters, that grace is not just theological construct, but becomes embodied in human hands. My questions do not get answered, nor is pain relieved, but for a moment I find hope. That one child would be held, who would not otherwise know tenderness, this mattered immensely as I stood on the Bucharest pavement, silent in my tears.

REMOVED FROM HAZEROTH IVAN FAUTE

"The dancing show isn't the same without you chicky," Clyde would say to her as he passed with the steaks and kidneys for the cats. "You were always the one they came to see." Miriam knew it already. To see him walking by with a metal pan full of cow-flesh and telling her this, she thought about that dead ring in the white cool room. Miriam was lying on her back, left side exposed. Around her breast they had drawn a circle with a wax crayon like a bull's-eye. The drugs took effect and she felt no pain, but knew everything, knew the scalpel removing her flesh and the nurse helping pull away the fibers. Suddenly, she was lighter and sewn together and scarred.

Clyde didn't fire her, because she was part of the family. "We are all part of a family, babe," he said. "We take care of our own. You can help us take care of those llamas and goats and shit. All those useless animals, but the kids love them. What can you do?"

She could no longer dance. Her costumes were made to cling to her body. Her flesh, flowing and rippling just out of reach of the men, something underneath her skin afraid of the touch of those rough fingers. Fingers with deep ridges of work, the swirls frozen into hard crusts by lifting and pushing.

She explained her dancing to her mother that way, when her mother was still alive, laid out straight as a board on the hospital bed. Belly dancing isn't sex dancing, Miriam said. It isn't get up on the table and show them what you've got. It's all fantasy, and the almost, and the always pulling back before it gets to touching, she would say. Her mother, unable to move anything but the ends of her body, the tips of her fingers and her eyes, and able to pucker her mouth like a child trying to offer a kiss, stared. She blew on her mother's arm, the elbow locked in place, and the white, thin hairs stood up on end, one set on the top of each goose pimple. Like that, she'd said to her mother, it's just like that feeling. And you can feel that tingle all the way up your arm, back into the sides of your brain.

Clyde let her do anything that was faceless. She wore flannel shirts and heavy sweatshirts, and with her fooling bra, like she called it, and without her sparkles and eye makeup, no one cared that she wasn't complete, like she called it. Miriam unpacked, packed up, swept, and busied herself so that she was less a hard worker than a blur, smudge of someone moving past, leaving cleanliness, completed tasks behind.

A MASTECTOMY MEANT SLICING OFF A PORTION OF HER BODY, throwing it away like some rotten meat. The harsh consonant stuck in Miriam's ear and comforted her because it was so final, so evil, like the sickle of Time moving across the land cutting down those commanded him by God. After they cut off Miriam's breast, they placed it in a stainless steel kidney pan. The doctor examined it a little, poking it with his finger, pushing aside a long, pink fiber that twisted under and around itself. The nurse attached a pre-made label and sent it off to the lab. They took out the blue, metallic looking muscle that wrapped up around her shoulder and then the yellow, lumpy lymph nodes under her armpit. They gathered skin together and, after pinning it, the intern sewed it shut.

They told her it was impossible for her to remember these events when she'd said she could; her unconscious would be complete, deep, amnestic. Miriam did remember all of it. She felt the slick, heated knife, the cauterizing scalpels that sealed her as they opened her body, the gentle touch of the physician as he held her breast tenderly by the hard, puckered end of the nipple. Perhaps the removal of her bodily tissue was more than just cutting off her fingernails or her hair, the way the doctor described it to her. He told her about the small tumors, showed her x-rays and diagrams, everything done abstractly and concisely. "The cancer is in stage three. We call the mastectomy 'local treatment.' A simple operation. And the systemic treatment will be the chemotherapy and hormone therapy."

Miriam liked information presented this way. Without pretense or sympathy or feeling when no feeling or sympathy was there. She knew he didn't care, could read people, and when she knew something, she would rather it without that veil. Being in show business had put her off acting; she liked reason and immaculate fact.

Measurable things, like the sound her flesh made against the bottom of that steel container. A dull, low ring when the physician tossed her breast into the pan, the sound slipping about that room with its hard-scrubbed, brown linoleum tiles and dropped ceiling. At any time, her mind was ready to lift that sound up out her memory and let it rest, like a drop of water, inside the hollow bottom of her ear. Most of the day, she worked, forgot about that noise, that hospital stay, and the fact that she no longer had two breasts. Most of the day, she was sweeping and feeding, or repairing costumes, or selling tickets, solving problems about schedules, and explaining why who went where. She focused on the tasks before her, and these little things, activities, entwined themselves to make a barrier to memory, to the body.

* * *

"The chemo will make you very ill, but it is essential because of the nature of the lumps. It is especially important that you continue to eat well. We find that those who make a concerted effort at eating right, and stick to it, do better." This doctor was a woman. "The hormone treatments will be less trying. Mostly, your experience will be similar to menopause. Hot flashes and interrupted periods, but nothing too severe. Because of your age there really isn't much danger of sterilization or irreversible menopause, either." Pause. "Things really are going well."

All those heavy atoms flowing through her blood that they wouldn't allow to come near her otherwise, in the real world. And there they were, two bottles of toxic waste for Miriam to receive unto herself. Days, alone in her trailer, swallowing poisons that would cure, she then went out to work until it got so bad in Kentucky she was taken to the hospital. "You shouldn't work. It's the worst thing you can do. You should rest." I have to pay for these visits and these consultations, she'd said. "But don't you have relatives or friends you could stay with?" compassionate women would ask, shaking their heads side to side. I don't really know anyone, except circus people, and we all travel, she'd said. Then Tuesday morning, she moved on.

She didn't care about her hair; she'd never cared for it. It had all fallen out once before, when she tried to double color it at fifteen. "Better to be bald than look like a whore," her mother said, before she fell and wet herself. But that was later, when Miriam had two inches of brown fuzz sticking every which way and everyone thought she was a boy from behind.

It was so hard to eat. Three, four times a day, it all came up. Clyde, rarely compassionate, let her work four-hour shifts, after the shows. "Don't get used to it. It's just until you feel a little better," he'd said. She fed animals and cleaned up the elephant's waste, mixed in as it was with moldy hay.

Worst were the bruises that never healed. From carrying a water bucket on her arm or bumping into a wooden post, she could see the green and yellow flesh fill with blood, and it would grow and deepen for days or weeks. She worried about seeing huge purple and black islands in her always before satiny skin.

At the medical store, they were obeisant. The saleswoman referred to the loss of Miriam's flesh the same way she might talk about a haircut or some weight she'd lost. "I think that bra looks fine, very natural. And, of course, you can adjust the way it rests against your chest. Sometimes you might get a little sore or rash, especially at first." The woman scratched the air in front of her triangular lumps. "Eventually, the scar heals up and hardens a bit. My patients tell me they don't notice much. One woman even said she thought she looked better." Miriam's eyes were restless, along the wall hung three dozen legs, peach colored and dull chocolate, each one on a separate thin metal hook. All sizes, for thin people and some for fat. On the bottom of each dangled a foot, half a circle, flat on the bottom like half a sandwich roll covered in plastic and attached by a dull silver loop. She purchased just one bra, even though the saleswoman assured her most people liked to get at least two or three. The bra cost as much as she made in a week.

Later, when she'd bought the new brassier and consulted with the doctors one last time, they considered her healed and Clyde sent her out to work for real. She toted hay, carried buckets of water. The wind swarmed her face as she turned each corner of the fabric buildings being torn down or assembled. Her lips dried out and bled. She licked it off and tasted the salt. A strand of muddy-colored hair might sweep in and out of the moist corner of her eye.

The camels and llamas were kept together in one stall. At night, she measured out a quarter bale of hay and one cup of feed for each one. Clyde appreciated most her frugality, her precision, her responsibility. She still could control every muscle, each one in her body she could move independently of the other. Miriam divided the hay bales with precision and measured out grain with proficiency. "You do it like a dance," Clyde said. "You still move like a dancer," he said with a chuckle.

The gray and white llama wasn't due for several weeks, but as Miriam entered the pen, she heard an undulating bass sound. The animal stood in the middle of the pen. Black blood and thick, green mucous that had once encompassed her baby, covering her back legs. The three other llamas and the two camels, short for camels but towering over the other ruminants, tried to get close to investigate, to comfort their friend, but the mother kept them off, spitting at them between the spaces of her humming.

Miriam threw down some straw onto the mess and pushed it down, mixing it with the toe of her boot, like she was making bricks. Lifting her foot, the mucous stuck in a fat lump to her sole, linking her to the ground. It hung dangerously thin in the middle, and she tried to shake it free, break the connection between herself and the ground, but it refused and the viscous twisted in irregular loops.

The llama trusted Miriam. The animal let out a plaintive mew and then a sweet huff of air in greeting. Miriam blew back to say hello and, assured, the llama turned about. A tiny head, perfect replica of its mother, was held immobile by two legs like splints, topped with split hooves and evenly divided with the lumps of its knee joints. The cria gulped in air between its bleats, tasting for the first time oxygen not filtered through glucose and blood cells, testing its voice as well. The mother twirled about, twisting her head, trying to see what caused her so much pain, trying to reach the origin of that sound that she knew, somehow knew, to be her child, afraid. The adult bleated and sniffed and walked in circles, led by her nose, trying to catch her backside. Miriam grabbed the lean shoulders, and in one movement, the cria slid to the floor. The mother looked down, unsure, sniffed the head. The two exchanged huffs of breath and then, before she began to nibble off the remains of birth, the mother leaned over and with another exhalation blew the hair out of Miriam's eyes.

TWO SPIRITS DANIEL H. FAIRLY, JR.

I remember the false energy racing through my veins
My head reacting to every drum, light, and body
With unsuspicious, ecstatic passion and entrancement

I remember believing I'd found light through darkness
That I had entered heaven through hell
And scorning simple slogans learned at school

I remember love and un-summoned pleasure
And dancing, spinning smiles and lights—
The inner purity of being, un-strangled and free

I remember waking to hot sun through a windshield
At midday, with flashes of dismal mistakenness
Spotting those dread paths the drug had blessed

I remember feeling, physically, so far from peace
As if the Fall had materialized within me
I remember despair and depression and asking Jesus to come back
I remember believing He could not
I remember disturbed, frenzied emptiness

And the sickness of my own humanity—
Warped, deluded, and believing I
Had discovered something new under the sun

SAMHAIN SHUFFLE *(DANSE MACABRE)* JERRY SALYER

There's lights, there's camera, there's action
Mirror of internal, infernal shrieking of gears.
But pea-soup-thick rhythm sometimes fails to serve as distraction.
Could it be just this—simple mechanics' expression?
An often-repeated, never-learned lesson?

Em-one, vee-one, is em-two, vee-two—
There is no "we" to such program, such smooth calculation,
Such rule for the running of the billiard-ball nation.
Always this? Just kah-cough-any?
Will it always and ever get the better of the worst part of me?

(Just "I"
Over "You,"
Except before "why.")

Do you remember, long time ago
Daddy worked for a man called Cotton-Eyed Joe
Daddy worked for a man called Cotton-Eyed Joe

A tired, solemn golem of ashes-and-dust
An outdated datum
Can twitch, along to Brownian motion
Motion, finally end-less, at the heart of the Nature of Things
Things—like plankton—whose voices are drowned out by ocean.

But then I says to myself, "Self,
Don't mumble, maudlin, about oceans, you schizo."
For I've seen real oceans, and I've seen seas—long time ago.

SAMHAIN SHUFFLE (DANSE MACABRE)

Even more, I *remember* oceans, and I *remember* seas.
And I remember crumpled dying-duck jet fighter wings
Sending pillars of smoke from the waves, to brace the red roof of the world.
And foreign tongues' curses, lips snarling and curled,
And the wincing, flinching turning away
From the face-searing flickers of missiles at play.
And I remember waters colder and rougher than this.

I coulda been married, long time ago
If it hadn't a-been for Cotton-Eyed Joe
If it hadn't a-been for Cotton-Eyed Joe

And I remember algae-green-cheeked boys with quivering knees
Whose very hopes were bound to bounding oceans, exactly like this,
Exactly like these dark, blinding seas,
These puddles of life, where tequila dopes vein-wine with anti-freeze

(So the chill may be ignored.)

"Strawberry," "Dark Room," "L'Amnesia"
"The Axis," "Technomad," and "Sciusia"

Different names, same blurred spot,
Shady, indeterminate,
A great, grand, gilded box: but Schroedinger's wiser cat would never dream
Of being—or becoming—caught
Half-dead in it.

Old bull fiddle and a shoe-string bow
Wouldn't play nothing but Cotton-Eyed Joe
Wouldn't play nothing but Cotton-Eyed Joe

The proton, loosened, cannot avoid
The repulsive fate of ejection out into street-void.
For in times like these tying forces are rare
But recompense is made—as would be only fair.
Perhaps harmony is a cheap price for freedom,
(degree'd infinite)

JERRY SALYER

And perhaps Man's fear of Man is the beginning
Of the beginning of wisdom.
(But, brother, I doubt it.)

Play it fast or play it slow
Wouldn't play nothing but Cotton-Eyed Joe
Wouldn't play nothing but Cotton-Eyed Joe

So with all that in mind,
Could you be kind,
And tell me one thing, or two—my good Mr. Joe—
(His friends call him "Cotton")
Is there anything in now-times, here,
That won't be forgotten,
If I look away, look away, look away?

No, really; where do you come from, where do you go?
Where do you come from, where do you go?

HOW I EXPLAIN MY RELIGIOUS HISTORY AMBER HARRIS LEICHNER

He snaps his face toward mine, eyes rounded in disbelief,
the question more like an exclamation. *You've never been baptized?*
And then I think, *how wrong could it be if a mother*
thought it best her daughter find God on her own?
Then he asks, *Does it bother you?* while taking my hand.
I feel as mute and useless as a paper bell.

Once, my mother's stolen purse was found stuffed in the cup of a rusted bell.
So together we walked to the mission church to rescue her belief
in that Southwestern town. She never let go of my hand.
Ten bucks and a checkbook had vanished, a trivial start to our desert baptism.
That purse again dangled at her hip. *Yes*, she said, *we're on our own.*
I was four. I knew already why my father had left the baby, me, my mother.

I began to pray the year I lost my grandmother.
Among the tokens she left for me was a porcelain bell.
Only a week in my palm and I'd cracked its surface. I couldn't own
up to my clumsy guilt. But still the bell's quiet ringing meant belief,
meant that someone could hear my longing for baptism.
At night I whispered *forgive me*, a fragile handle inside my hand.

Later that year a friend's parents thought they could help me, hand
me over for salvation. They got permission from Mother
and bused me to Bible School. They didn't know I was unbaptized.
Ashamed, I hid my original sin and went passing under the church bells.
Fearing limbo, I had to outdo all the other children for belief.
So I memorized every verse—willed their truths to become my own.

At Notre-Dame I stood in a twenty year-old body—no longer my own—
trembled beneath the assault of glass and stone and so many hands.
They say such places put the fear of God in you, that they inflame belief.

AMBER HARRIS LEICHNER

No different, I stood in the nave only miles from the birthplace of my mother,
but somehow altered just enough to feel at home under the great bell
that called forth 900 years of Parisian baptisms.

Once I was given a catechism. It said *Baptism
is birth.* Over and over I read those words, my own
existence imploding. *It drives away the devil*—a line like a death-bell
to a little girl yearning for a pair of holy hands
that might scoop up her soul. I needed her then, my mother.
But I couldn't feel her arms across the chasm of my belief.

They say you need your own petition for faith. *Lord, I believe; help thou my unbelief.*
I've seen baptisms, saw two sisters in their bell-shaped dresses, damp
white ruffles. I saw a mother wade into a lake, her hands wipe her child's eyes.

TURNER'S SIN J. MARK BERTRAND

THE CHORUS

Turner's sin found its source neither in omission nor commission. If anything, it was a sin of recognition; more precisely, the failure to recognize what he had seen. The pastor of his small Baptist church might have told him it was no sin at all, but for Turner it carried the weight of sin and condemned him more surely than anything else he had done in life. Even the policeman who took Turner's statement, a man whose health was eventually broken by the inconclusive investigation, was inclined to think the deacon and university dean did protest too much. Turner's mistake was one anybody might make.

THE STATEMENT

—It must have been around eight-thirty, maybe closer to nine. The faculty meetings end at eight but sometimes there are fires I need to put out. This time it was . . . [*inaudible*] . . . angry about his departmental budget; he wanted an increase, but there was nothing I could do. He was lucky we hadn't cut it the way some of the others were.

—I'm sorry, but could we skip over the details of the meeting?

—Yes, of course, I apologize about that. You can see the power this stuff has; it's a constant preoccupation. So I left between eight-thirty and nine, and by that time the rain was coming down pretty hard. It started up during the meeting, a real storm blowing so hard you could feel it in the walls of the old building. I had to collect my umbrella from my office upstairs, though it didn't do any good and I was thoroughly soaked by the time I'd gotten to my car. Just as I was starting the engine, that's when Burke ran out and tapped on the window. To . . . [*inaudible*], which was gracious of him, and I don't think I was too gracious in return with all the water pouring in through the window. Anyway, I left. It must have been a few minutes before nine.

—And what route did you take?

—My usual one.

—Well, for the tape, could you elaborate on that?

—The route I usually take home runs around the back of the campus, behind the dormitories and the football field. There's a direct road to the highway from the main entrance, but since I live in Brushmore it's faster to go the back way. Only it isn't very well lit—that's been an issue for some time, but it's the city not us—so in a downpour you have to take it slow because of the curves. So that's what I was doing. The final curve before you reach the turnoff on Pike has the edge of the football field on one side and some woods on the other. That's where it happened.

—Are you all right? Are you okay to continue?

—Sure, of course. I'm . . . [*inaudible*].

—Sorry?

—It's just realizing, you know. That's where it happened, only I didn't see it. I mean, I *did* see it but I didn't see what it was.

—Can you describe what happened?

—My speed, it must have been twenty-five. The wipers were going and I was dripping wet myself. It was pitch black except for my headlights and they hardly seemed to be putting out any light at all. So I was hunched over the wheel struggling to see. I've always had this fear of sliding off the road right there, so I'm careful. Then suddenly, I saw something on the road ahead. I slammed on the brakes, jerked to a stop and only then did it register what I'd seen: a girl crossing the road.

—Did you see who it was? Could you describe how she was dressed?

—She was too far ahead for me to recognize, and moving too fast, running right along the edge of my lights. I think she was wearing shorts, or maybe a short skirt, because I remember the bright . . . [*inaudible*] . . . of the headlights on her legs. But that's all, really, and I only saw her for a moment before she . . . [*inaudible*].

—Can you speak up for the tape? Heading in what direction?

—Well, my impression was that she was crossing from the field into the woods.

—Sal, will you bring Dr. Turner something to drink. Coffee?

—I'm fine. I should have realized. I could have done something.

—You couldn't have done anything. You can't change what happened.

—But I was thinking how stupid these kids are, how you could get yourself killed crossing that road at night, and I love the kids, the students, you know, this is my life, what I do, but you get frustrated and having to slam the brakes on and have my briefcase spill onto the floor I was angry and I was thinking what kind of idiot would be out here in the middle of a rainstorm at night. It never even occurred to me to get out of the car.

—Why should it have?

—Because of the boy. Because right after that, before I could even take my foot off the brake, I saw him crossing over, too. Denim jacket, black hair—or maybe it was wet, I don't know. I wasn't paying attention. I was irritated and I kept driving and told myself there needed to be some kind of notice to students about that road. And all that time. Do you think . . . [inaudible], right then?

—Not long after. She'd been dead for twelve hours by the time they found her.

—Oh, . . . [inaudible].

THE SEAL OF THE CONFESSIONAL

Turner isn't a legalist necessarily, or not what I would call one. But grace is more something in his vocabulary than his experience, if you see what I mean. There's this phase, you know, that children go through, when they're first coming to understand about sin. Whenever they do something wrong—even something that's trivial, that you wouldn't even consider worth mentioning—there's this wellspring of innocent guilt and they confess in tears, like they'd just killed somebody when all they did was take an extra piece of gum. Turner's kind of like that. He doesn't give himself many breaks. If we were Catholics he would spend a lot of time in the confessional. Not to save himself, though; more to clear his conscience. He has that same thing, that innocent guilt.

His wife is a sweet lady and she said something that sums Turner up pretty good: she said he shoulders guilt the way he shoulders responsibility. He makes himself accountable for things that are really outside his control.

"Now Turner," I told him, "how long have I known you? And in all that time would you say I struck you as a good judge of character? Well, here's my judgment of your character. You're a good man, a man saved by grace, but you don't know how to leave your burden at the cross. You always want to take it up again."

I could see this wasn't what he wanted to hear. The funny thing is, he'll know what you're gonna tell him and he'll come to you all the same. What *could* I tell him? He was making himself miserable, making that sweet lady miserable, driving everyone crazy with this spirit of self-condemnation, and all I could tell him was to let it go. You confess your sin—if it even is a sin—and God forgives it, and you move on. Turner knows that, but he struggles with it. And part of me, I have to say, part of me kind of admires his struggle.

If he didn't take it so far.

HER OUTBOX

June 3. He says he offered his resignation and they're considering it. Not because they want him to, but because he won't leave it alone. Now that the semester is over I want it all to go away. I feel like I hate him, I hate everyone, I hate the girl who went off like that and the boy who should rot in hell and I hate that he had to see what he saw and I hate that they told him if he had only come forward or done something. It's me that should resign and get out of this. Doing what she did, or what was done to her, ended my life, too. . .

Later. Okay, that was melodramatic. Ignore that last one. I sound like a bad person. That's the problem I guess; I make myself out to be a bad person but I know I'm not, and he thinks he is and doesn't know he isn't. Only there are things he does that I want to tell him, stop it—but with him blowing everything out of proportion like this, I keep thinking that if I say a word he's going to jump off a bridge or something. Did I marry this man? Was he like this? I don't know anymore . . .

June 7. Well that is that.

June 23. I guess you've heard? According to Pastor Mike the rest of the deacons were stunned. They said afterwards there must be a deeper problem, and I know that's why he called, to see if I would tell him. A deeper problem, because no one could leave his job and leave his position in the church just for standing by while a nineteen-year-old girl is raped and beaten to death and you do nothing. You don't even notice. Who gives everything up just for not noticing?

Today. I really don't think I can take it anymore. I'll call you from the road. I have to get away from here or I'll . . .

ET IN ARCADIA EGO

On the second floor balcony a tall gray-haired man in rimless glasses and a crisp tan raincoat regards the campus view. He is a fastidious dresser who speaks with precision and, in spite of being an administrator (that is, a former administrator), looks more like the Platonic ideal of the academic than the generations of real academics who have cursed and blessed him over the years. His eyes glisten, reflecting back a speckled version of the view.

This is Arcadia, he tells himself. *Or Eden.*

And me the serpent? More like the worm.

Turner is here to hand over the keys, so to speak. The search was half-hearted and in the end the university promoted one of its own, so there was nothing for Turner to do aside from offering his congratulations and a word or two at the ceremony that has just finished. Now his duties are discharged and he can take a moment to look at what he's left behind.

"Resigning won't help anything," Lou Purcell had told him. With no suspect after four and half months, Lou wasn't in the mood to comfort anyone. He just wanted to voice his opposition for the record. That was before the big man's stroke, brought on by stress from the job and, according to the doctors, a prodigious amount of salt.

But it does help, and that's what no one else will understand. Turner can never explain it, though he has tried. *The detective thinks I'm too smart to see what's obvious, the preacher thinks it's a crisis of faith and my wife wants to believe I'm doing all of this to get at her. They're convincing, too. They make me wonder about myself.*

He leaves that spot on the balcony and takes the back stairs down to the exit. From there he walks across the courtyard between the university's original red brick buildings, a scenic but inconvenient path he rarely took in the far off days of last spring and all the years that preceded them.

To go through something like that and not be changed . . . that's what they expected of him. And Turner can't say in what way he *should* change, only that he has to, that he refuses to let the experience leave him unmarked. What had been an inconvenience must become a transformation or what would it say about him? A man on whom experience is lost is . . . lost.

This is Turner's farewell procession. He feels light, almost buoyant, like he wants to fight but not in earnest, yearning to prove himself, to test his skill.

Not a dean any longer or a deacon, either. Not a man staked down and settled under the world's weight. He has destroyed himself to be free.

Am I now a man who would stop everything, who would enter the rain, a man who would give chase?

MORTISE AND TENON CHAD GUSLER

By the time you find this I'll probably be somewhere in Illinois, maybe near Kankakee, hopefully farther. Sorry about taking the car, by the way, but I figured that since it has been me who has nursed it along these past years you wouldn't mind. You could always take your tractor to town. Don't you find that ironic, you driving a tractor, considering that it was my side of the family that farmed, not yours? And how laughable is it that you're a farmer and a vegetarian! I still can't help thinking that your sudden interest in farming was your attempt to fit in with my banausic relatives. Deny it if you must, but you know my argument. We've been over that hundreds of times.

I should also mention that there's no use in trying to pursue me. This is as sudden for me as it is for you, so I really don't have a destination—west is all I know. And don't bother with a credit card search: I'm only carrying cash. I've left the credit cards on the desk next to your humidor and bourbon.

It should be a good day for traveling—sunny and in the mid-seventies according to the Weather Channel—and I suspect you'll be picking corn. Please think of me as you bounce along in your torn tractor seat, and when you come inside for a beer and find this note taped to the refrigerator, don't fret. In fact, pour yourself a whiskey chaser. Sit in the sun. Breathe in that God-green air of mown grass and smile. It's not the end of the world. In fact, I'm still with you. I'm the vestigial woman who floats silently through the hallways of our unfinished house. But don't take me as an eidolon, and for God's sake don't fear. Now that sounds like the pastor you know and love so well, doesn't it? Always positive! Always cheerful! Generous! Giving! Selfless! It's what every minister should be.

I know you're full of questions. Some I can answer, some I cannot, and hopefully some will become clearer as I write. Four nights ago we had Mark and Lori over for dinner. You were in peak form that night: cordial, funny, smart, and—flutter! flutter!—so very sexy with that clean-shaven face of yours. You impressed them with your *coq au vin*. I know this because Lori pulled me aside while we were cleaning up and you were showing Mark your workshop, and she told me in a rather breathy voice how lucky I was to have a man like you, someone who is both adept in the kitchen and in the field. And how very brave of you to allow meat in your precious kitchen! Bravery—that's a manly trait. She's right, of course; I am lucky, and that makes this letter all the more difficult to write, for what sane woman would ever leave a man like you?

After you fell asleep, I retreated back downstairs and sat at the kitchen table, finishing the bottle of wine with Sammy curled up on my lap. The radio forfeited *The Blues Room* for folk music, and as I sat there with my wine glass and listened to lonely men with guitars and harmonicas sing about love or peace or the Intifada or terrorism, I thought of our wedding. Can you believe it will be almost fourteen years? Somewhere in this mess we have a cassette tape of our wedding, and I must confess that in my drunken state I managed to locate it. You slept soundly through the whole ordeal of my pulling down the cranky attic steps to search through our several boxes full of eighties' music. The attic was still warm from the long-gone sun, and I lingered up there even after I had found the tape wedged between your saintly U2 and my much bespattered Cyndi Lauper. I moved to the living room and listened to the tape. Do you remember the preacher's homily? It was simple, yet profound—as a good sermon should be—and he could always say much with few words. I think in our hard-ass determination to have a wedding homily not based on the dilapidated chapter of love in First Corinthians we got more than we wrangled for by using Ephesians 4:15-16. How much easier would it have been to have a wedding sermon based on love is patient and kind, never jealous, arrogant, rude, resentful, et cetera, et cetera, et cetera. No. Instead we got "speaking the truth in love, we are to grow up in every way into Christ, from whom the whole body, joined and knit together by every joint with which it is supplied, when each part is working properly, makes a bodily growth and upbuilds itself in love." His short sermon was lovely, and I found his metaphor striking. Marriage is like the church, the body of Christ, he said, and it seems to me that marriage is beyond love, that it lies in a different realm. That's a lot to live up to, don't you think?

I lay awake in bed for some time. You were warm, and while I pressed my feet against your legs I hung my hand over the edge of the bed and stroked the bed frame, jerking it away after I got a splinter in my middle finger. I never realized how rough it was underneath. I guess Grandpa Wenger never sanded the hidden parts. And now here I sit, typing, my finger hurting whenever I hit the i, k, or comma key. Such a tiny thing, and yet my body is pushing it out, not able to tolerate so small a foreign visitor.

The next morning I rolled over onto your side of the bed. You hadn't been gone long because I could still smell you in your pillow. I sat up, pulled away the shades from the window, and stared out into the gray, drizzly morning. Little madid clouds, in a desperate attempt to hang themselves out to dry, twisted and twirled around the clothesline and your lone sodden sock. I realized that I had forgotten to move the laundry from the machine to the line yesterday. (That's why your load of jeans next to the dresser smells a little funky.)

Bless you for making coffee. What a surprise to come bedraggling into the warm kitchen and see a hot pot waiting in the gleaming Cuisinart. It was strange to see your work boots in the kitchen pointing neatly towards the refrigerator. Were you raptured away, your vegetarian God leaving your leather-free boots in your stead? Sammy rubbed against them after he finished cleaning out your cereal bowl, and you came banging in through the mud room soon after, soggy hair plastered to your face, cut grass growing from your wet feet.

"It's beautiful," you said.

I think I moaned then refilled my cup.

"No, it really is. It's actually kind of warm."

"And I suppose Chicago was never like this," I said. You're always complaining about cold Chicago.

"Well, we had our heat waves and all, but this is different. This drizzle is warming and cooling at the same time."

"That doesn't make any sense."

"See for yourself," you said, sitting down with some coffee.

"I've got laundry that's going to stink if I don't put in the dryer soon."

"You've always got laundry."

"Yes, and?"

"I don't mind wearing my clothes for weeks at a time."

"Okay, but I do."

Your Adam's apple bobbed up and down while you laughed.

"What's up with your boots?" I asked.

"I decided not to wear them. Surprised?"

"I'm more amused than surprised."

"I wanted to feel the wet grass under my toes, to feel connected with the dirt," you said.

"O worthy farmer, I bow in your presence," I said.

"Hey, if they bothered you, you could've moved them." You were never good with sarcasm. I really didn't mean to upset you. Blame me on the gloomy weather, but why did you get so upset?

Can you believe this? I actually listened to one of your CDs. After you left for town I rummaged through your music collection labeled "Experimental," and I found Brian Eno. Providential? I'd say yes, though I'm sure you'd say coincidence. It was called "Landscape with Haze," and I was enthralled. What a perfect song for a dank day. Can you imagine me writing sermons to that sort of stuff? Church attendance would dwindle, though maybe I'd connect with a few of those wayward Mennonite goth kids that hang out at McDonald's. Anyway, Eno's synthesizers created a sordid brume that enveloped me for the rest of the day; really, all the way until this morning when some semblance of the sun flopped through the Godforsaken sky and meekly lit the dewy grass with Crayola yellow.

So I skipped my sermon writing (thank you, Brian Eno) and thought about seminary, which seems forever ago, but I remember seeing you sitting on a bench at the park, stacks of your graduate school books at your side, a dull pencil resting snugly behind your ear. It was an early Virginia spring, and kids swarmed the playground in their bare feet. We studied while sock-less children flitted around the monkey bars. I sat across the playground from you. Do you remember? Your boots seemed bolted into the ground, more a part of the dirt than something man-made, and were all the more impressive in comparison with the quick-footed children. It took you long enough to notice me, but when you did, you smiled and clomped over.

"Are you religious or something?" you asked, looking through my New Testament textbook.

"Everyone's religious in their own way," I said.

"Yeah, I guess. You want a beer?" You took me downtown for some pints and gyros. You watched me in wonderment as I gormandized my meat and Guinness, and I laughed at you, my lonely vegetable eater, while you prodded and herded your veggie pita into your mouth.

I put Eno away, arranged your music, and looked out the window. The sky hadn't yet lifted above the craggy oaks in the front yard, and the drizzle had turned into fine, steady rain. I took off my shoes, placed them where your boots had been, and walked out into the wet grass. I wanted to feel what you felt, to sense the world as you, but I only got annoyed at the cut grass that stuck to my feet and ankles. Your wood shop was warm and I could see why you retreat to your shed so often—it's a haven. I guess I can't blame you for being hesitant on my wanting a work space out there: I wouldn't want intruders either. The Makita girl smiled down on me from your calendar. Where'd you get that thing anyway? I know you didn't get it from Stolzfus Hardware. There's no way in hell that that bimbo in half a shirt even knows where the switch is to that miter saw. So go ahead and tease me about Jude Law; I don't care. At least he has some class.

I saw your bookshelf—is that your current recherché project?—in the corner next to the trash can. It's astonishing how good of a woodworker you've become. Are you sure there's not a Mennonite bone in that agnostic body of yours? You even sanded the back of the piece. I must say, though, that Grandpa Wenger would be appalled that you wasted so much precious time in finishing something unseen. At least your wood didn't splinter into my finger. Thank you. I found your broom and swept a clean ring onto the dirty floor on which I could do a little yoga, but the swish of the broom made such a pleasant sound, and the aroma released from the fluttering shavings of oak and pine so welcome, that I swept your whole shop and didn't bother with the yoga. I've never felt so invigorated. I hung the broom on the center beam opposite the old bent nail that held three of your walnut picture frames. I suppose I should be thankful that you sanded them given my current splinter and my lift from sweeping dust and shavings off the floor, but I can't help but think that you're trying to erase yourself. I took down a frame from the nail, the smallest frame, and looked for signs of you. Your mortise and tenon joints were almost seamless. Such violence in fastening, so rape-like, yet so smooth—what a fine frame for a wedding picture. I imagine a happy couple, conjoined at the waist and lips, inseparable with beatific, giddy smiles. I picture you as I write: air hose in hand with compressor-churned air, you sweeping your nozzle from side to side, dust violently thrown from your newly-sanded wood, motes stranded in gusting air, crashing into each other like superheated electrons, and you smiling. There was no trace of you on the frame, almost as if it were created in a factory somewhere. You don't have to be so selfish! You can share your prints with me.

The maple by the back door threw its wet, leafy greens in my face when I came back inside. I ate a roast beef sandwich, then lay on the couch and masturbated. I thought of your vinyl boots and came quickly, a rather lackluster moment, really, done to prove to myself that I'm not the innocent little Mennonite girl your family so lovingly takes me as. You arrived soon, and I tidied up the house, made some soup, and complained about sermon writing while we ate.

Brenda called while I was doing the dishes, and we chatted for some time, long after I had dried them and put them away. You were in your shop.

"And?" You hung another picture frame on a nail and wiped your hands on a threadbare rag.

"I'm going out tonight," I said.

"You never go out with me anymore."

"I don't go out at all anymore."

"I didn't think you liked going out."

"You never ask me."

"But you're a homebody," you said.

"Preacher girls like beer, too," I said.

"So where you going?"

"Nowhere fancy."

"Well, that's a surprise," you said, draining the air from your compressor. It hissed wildly.

"We're going to the Pub in Goshen," I said.

Did you know that they have a fantastic selection of eighties music on their jukebox? Lots of U2, even some Bruce Cockburn and R.E.M., but what we played—and let me tell you, we played it without trepidation!—was Cyndi Lauper and Boy George, Madonna and Quiet Riot. We drank two pitchers of Pabst, danced a little, got hit on by some young college boys (which was flattering, though they were probably relatives of mine), and ate a plate of diablo nachos. Keep pushing—they may serve organic beer someday. Brenda shared her cigarettes, and we talked until they kicked us out. You stirred when I crawled into bed. I kissed your dry, cracked lips and you puffed your cheeks; your breath was sibilant, a curled-up snake wanting rest, warning me not to wake it.

You left me no coffee the next morning, just a sink holding a chipped mug and crusty bowl. I opened the window above the sink to let in the freshly-washed air and as I did, I knocked over the little photograph of you sitting on the sill. The frame broke when it hit your tile counter, and the glass shattered into your ceramic sink. I pulled the picture from the frame. It was the one of you taken before your family moved to Chicago, the one of you standing on the porch of a clapboard house in front of a screen door, a little towhead boy wearing a plaid jacket, blue shorts, and red knee socks. I remember your description of that house, the way you tilted your head back and half smiled, your eyes closed while extracting animate memories, but it didn't seem to match what I saw. In the photograph the paint is peeling on the siding, and the screen is ripped, its hinges draining rust down the door frame. Where is the tidy house you so often coaxed from your head? Or is your recall not that good? I slipped the picture into my shirt pocket. I have it now, a memento of you and your memory, but maybe sometime soon I'll send it back and you could frame it properly then hang it in your bedroom.

I heard your tractor somewhere, maybe in the trees beyond the corn field. I made some tea, and when I went for the cream I saw your note on the refrigerator. You were in the woods, splitting oak with the hydraulic maul: "preparing our home for winter," you wrote. You said you'd be back for lunch. Tea is so halfhearted compared to coffee.

I actually composed a sermon that morning. I sat on the porch swing with a quilt across my lap and wrote on a blank page in one of your cookbooks. The winter root recipes must have been the cause of my afflatus. The oracle at Endor was so gracious to Saul when she offered a terrified man some food. Who wouldn't be aghast at the foretelling of their own death? She killed the calf, made some crackers, and told him he better eat because she said so. Isn't that so human, so woman, preparing a meal to make everything better? I should know: your food is soothing to me. Poor Saul. A grumpy Samuel told him that God had become his adversary, that God had become a satan to him, and that he would fall to the Philistines. What's a dispirited person to do? At least he didn't run away. He fulfilled his fate like a good flawed character should. The sermon's entitled Desperation, and it's in one of your cookbooks.

At lunch you found me in the laundry room with a box of wool socks.

"What's for lunch?" you asked.

"Look in the fridge," I said. "You're the cook."

"Leftovers it is, then. You know how to reheat, don't you?"

"Yes, but do you know how to darn a sock?"

You stared at me for a bit, then turned and went to the kitchen where I heard you banging stuff around.

The afternoon was warm and cloudy, and you stayed put in the woods till dark. I did my pastoral rounds at Greencroft. The old folks I visited asked about you, the ladies particularly. I told them you were fine, just fine, simply enjoying country life, he is, not a bone in his frame misses that smelly Chicago, though he's sad he can't see his family more, and he does miss the beer—did I really say that?—and pizza, but he's enjoying carpentry and farming and wood cutting and eating at *Das Essenhaus*. You get the idea. And me? How am I? No one asked, so I really couldn't tell you.

I refused your amorous moves that night, which I'm sure you remember, and hugged a bottle of wine instead. It was good, and I slept fitfully on the couch.

Let me tell you about the journeyman painter. I don't know where he's from, but there he was, on I-70, just outside Lawrence, Kansas, sitting on a barstool at Jed's Truck n' Wash. This was last February. It was cold, and I was on my way to Hesston for a meeting. He was eating cherry pie, and his black-specked hands trembled as he put the fork in his mouth. A rag hung from a loop in his painter's pants that were no longer white. His shoes were spotless.

I sat down next to him and ordered a Salisbury steak. "What's with the shoes?"

"Spit bath shiny," he said, lifting his rag. He had cherry filling on his scruffy chin. I pointed at it and he wiped it on the back of his hand.

"Where are you painting?"

He took a sip of coffee. "At the university. They're putting in a new theater. Black ceiling." He scraped at one of speckles of paint with his fingernail. "I sprayed it on. Got a new Graco in the back of my van. Had to use a wide tip. You know that acrylic paint eats the hell out of those tips. Fifty bucks a shot for one fucking tip."

"Where's your crew?"

"Just me. I search out the work, undercut the big boys, work, then take the cash and drive someplace else."

"You sleep in your van?"

"Sometimes, yeah. Though last night I hid in the theater and waited for everybody to leave. I slept next to my sprayer and laid the hose on my chest, coiled it like a snake, and together we watched the sky."

"The sky?"

"Yeah—the big black nighttime sky, freshly painted by me. No stars or moon. No falling sun. Just the night sky. I sleep best in the dark."

I finished my meal while Tim stood in the corner with a pinball machine. "You want to see my van?" he asked after I paid my bill.

His van was in the farthest slot from the building. The blacktop trembled as the semis idled. His van was white, though the rear bumper was streaked with different colors. It smelled like paint thinner inside, and he had a coffee maker perched on a stack of canvas drop cloths.

"This is where I keep my latex brushes," he said, pulling a plastic box from a shelf.

"Are those for oil paint?"

"These?" He pulled another box of black bristled brushes down.

"Yes."

"For oil paints and stains." He climbed between the seats, moved a coffee cup from the passenger seat, and patted it. I followed.

"Check this out," he said. Van Halen suddenly filled his van, and Tim played along beautifully with his air guitar. "Awesome system!" he hollered. He lit a cigarette, and I declined the one he offered. I don't think they were organic.

"It's amazing," I said.

He turned it off. "You in sales or something?"

"I'm a preacher," I said.

He laughed. "Same thing."

"How's that?"

"Just like a quack door-to-door salesman. The love you sell is no better than a trinket from the gum ball machine at fucking Wal-Mart. Sometimes you can get those claws to grab what you want, and sometimes they just close up in the empty air."

"I'm not like that," I said.

"You mean you'd give me a refund?" He flicked his cigarette out the window.

"Sure, and I'd see if you could exchange Jesus for the Buddha."

You, my agnostic love, would have applauded my performance in his stinky van. He reached under his seat and offered me Pabst in a can. I said no, told him that I had to be on my way. He drank the beer without talking, then leaned over and kissed me. I let him, then said goodbye and ran back to my car. When I turned around, his van was gone. Later that evening I had to bite my lip to keep from laughing when the conference minister prayed that "all would be touched with the love and forgiveness of Jesus."

You were still asleep yesterday when I flopped out of bed. I made coffee and sat on the porch with my mug and a ready wave for the Amish clopping by. One kid with blond bangs flashed me a furtive peace sign through his blurry buggy window. I was reminded of Tim as I watched Fritz direct a crew of painters around his barn. One painter extended a ladder and began scraping while the other two stood below mixing paint and smoking cigarettes and scanning the cloudy morning sky for rain. The cows stared at the men, and Fritz's wife oversaw them all through the slats in the window blinds. I occasionally caught a waft of her cinnamon rolls. When Fritz looks through his cracked spectacles at Alma does he feel devotion for her? Is it really possible to grow elderly and continue to love each other? I hear your answer: just ask them. I'm sure they'd say yes, but I don't know if I'd believe them. Tim drifts across the country, afloat in his van, unattached to anything but his sprayer—oh is he in love with it!—and he seems content to be accountable only to himself. I, on the other hand, wake up thinking of your day and how it will fit with mine: I wonder when you'll be home, when you'll need your shirts that I'm letting pile up next to the washing machine, when you'll want my affection, or if you'll need my help in the field. This is not contentment.

"Over easy?"

"Yes."

You flipped my egg, then slid it like a pro between two slabs of your toasted wheat bread.

"Here's the pepper."

"Thanks." I lifted the top slice of bread, peppered my egg, then replaced it. We ate quietly. You read the paper, and I watched your eyes scan every page. You looked at me twice in the thirty minutes we sat there. Do you feel love for me?

Oh wait . . . I shouldn't have to ask that.

Sorry.

When you returned to the woods, I took a few books, a pile of paper, some pencils, and a week's worth of clothes and packed them in my suitcase. I hid it in the trunk, and I must divulge that I was alarmed when you later took the car into town to get a few bags of potting soil. What luck I should have that you threw them in the back seat instead of the trunk! The gods are affable.

They're giving me the go ahead.

I went to the Blue Gate for lunch. A bus of Asian tourists with cameras was unloading when I cycled into the parking lot. I leaned my bike against a column on the front porch facade and ducked into the restaurant. I was halfway through my wiggle glacé and baked limas when Irvin Beachy picked me out from across the dining room.

"You look lonesome," he said, easing himself into the chair across me.

I put my book down. "No, not really. Just eating a little lunch."

"It's a good place to eat." He looked at my plate.

"Yes, it is."

"You got a good sermon this week?" He leaned back and put his arm on the back of the empty chair next to him.

"I hope so. It's about Saul."

"A true man of God."

"No. The other one. In the Old Testament."

Irvin thought a bit, then said, "Oh! He wasn't such a good guy, though I suppose the Lord left him in the Bible to show us how not to be."

I didn't tell him that I was friendly toward Saul, that I was pissed at David's carnivorous God Almighty.

"Well I just saw you sitting here and wanted to tell you what a fine preacher you are. We don't say thanks enough." Irvin stuck a toothpick in his mouth and limped to the cashier. I finished my lunch, and when I went to pay, the girl behind the register told me that my lunch had been paid for. Can you believe that? Someone paid me to eat meat!

When I returned home, you were in your shop planing some heart pine. Our conversation was of no account: the weather, my outing for lunch, your scheme for Sunday dinner, and your plans for the evening (beer and blues in Elkhart with your friends).

And this is what a goodbye sounds like: gravel crunching under your feet; Simon's car door slamming shut and the dull thud of bass rattling his Kia's frame; Sammy caterwauling at a opossum; the hum of your refrigerator; the scream of your teapot. You came home late and crashed into bed, and though you reeked of beer, I kissed you anyway. You didn't move.

It's early morning. You'll be sleeping in. Please answer the phone when they call tomorrow from church. It will be Irvin on the line. Tell him as much as you can. Tell him Saul was an okay guy.

CONVERSION MAUREEN DOYLE MCQUERRY

My father made me bracelets of smoke,
thin white strands that vanished in the slightest breeze.
I waited mannequin-still for his slow, round exhale,
for elegance to encircle me like the wide leather belt
that wrapped all twenty three inches of my mother's waist,
white gloves, pearl buttons, a Mrs. Mineva rose blooming
on her hat, the scarlet sunrise of her lips.

They went to nightclubs in New York,
danced to slow jazz, bubbles and smoke
rising with music into the canopied ceiling.
I've seen the pictures—movie star poses,
bathing suits in Mexico, New Years at Benny Hahn's
in San Francisco, taffeta or silk, tailored,
every pleat pressed, onyx-studded cufflinks;
she ironed his underwear.
No wonder church potluck dinners were foreign,

dishes of casserole, banana Jell-o
not one cocktail in the mix.
Reconcile these: Wednesday night basement suppers,
with pickled herring, lox on pumpernickel.
Sometimes the common ground is spare,
sharp as stubble in the corn fields
where a flannel graph shepherd stands,
in this picture nothing feels like home.
The words we knew, mystery and sacrament,
smelled of incense, flickered like candlelight.
We were lost in the translation.

HOLLOWS MAUREEN DOYLE MCQUERRY

The ravine is a deep cleavage,
a dry wrinkle in the shrub steppe

where riotous phlox, Carrie's Balsam Root and stiff
blue sentries of lupine war for moisture,

there is never enough, but scarcity can fool the eye.
This gully surges like a wadi at flood time,

full and frothing, a torrent of tumbleweeds
that traveled parched miles to fill the empty spaces,

to become a river whose source is wind
and seed. Search and you can find life

fighting its way up the gray stream, jumping like fish
in the shallows, lizards, scorpion, vole, they too collect

in empty places. We kneel,
dipping our hands into that which is not water,
how quickly our palms fill, like all the hollows of this world.

HOMING PIGEON MAUREEN DOYLE MCQUERRY

Cold rain on the car hood,
        rat-a-tat-tat of January's fire against the roof
of his silver Pontiac in the drive, McCabe's retreat
        after his wife and the pigeon man, three or four times a year

a sleek Ranchero delivers bundles of wooden crates and pebble-eyed
        messenger birds with oil slick wings,
rainbows sliding across black sheen, and every time,
        McCabe spends the night slouched in the Pontiac's front seat

smoking, listening to tunes, the red pinpoint
        of his ash a signal in the dark, thinking about his birds,
messages he will send, tied to their yellow scaled feet,
        unfolds a cigarette paper, in a cramped hand writes

words he rolls and slips in a tube, sky-bound words.
        Tomorrow they will rise flapping, into clouds or sun
heading for someone else's life, even 600 miles is not too far,
        in all the wide, tumultuous sky, it's his voice

carried and this night, bitter rain and glistening,
is such a small space, only a loft, a perch,
        one roost.

BOOKSHELVES KAREN MIEDRICH-LUO

> "I do not know what I may appear to the world; but to myself I seem to have been only a [child] playing by the seashore, and diverting myself in now and then finding a smoother pebble or a prettier shell than ordinary, whilst the great ocean of truth lay all undiscovered before me."
> —Sir Isaac Newton, *Memoirs of Newton*

A FOLDER IN MY FILE CABINET names every book I owned the year I left to teach English in China. It is an eclectic list, a map of all my rabbit trails, a compass by which I can locate who I was then by the books I read. I glance over the list remembering the pristine white shelves they sat on and it is like running my fingers across the bindings of my life. Here the novels and allegories I loved in high school nestle against the tomes of philosophy and ancient languages from the years of studying for a career in archaeology. Here lists books from a poorly timed attempt at a Master's degree in Literature where I grappled with the poets, playwrights and critics. Last are the grief books from the decade spent digging in the ruins of a broken marriage, trying to make sense of the death of my only child. And there the list ends. I could no longer focus on ephemeral pursuits any more than I could bring my life back from the dead. The books were shelved and ornamented with tasteful baubles—the shells of memory—to remind me I lived in a tangible world.

It took a few years for grief to subside, for the numbing effect of a reinvented life to weave a protective cocoon. I changed churches, found new friends, and bought a house. I had a job, a dog and a cat. I was content to slowly close the chapter of that last decade. Yet, so thorough a shelter did I construct that it threatened to bury me in mindless comfort. I needed something different, something so challenging that it would bring blood, the élan vital, back into my heart. An adolescent dream of working in another culture still pulled at my sleeves so I took a yearlong leave of absence from my job, family, friends, and pets, and decided to teach English in China.

I spent hours reorganizing my life and tying up loose ends. Andrea, a new housemate, agreed to watch the house and the pets until I returned the following year. Recently unemployed, she would make a good substitute while I was away. Like a thousand-piece puzzle, the intricacies of my world neatly began to fit into inter-locking painted spaces that would keep the semblance of my life in one-dimensional order while I disappeared behind the bamboo curtain.

Andrea had no interest in my books, but something about the notion of her living my life for one year had begun to addle my id. Perhaps I felt the need to take something with me to China that would remind me who I was, how I got to be there, who I was becoming. Something only your bookshelf can reveal. Reasoning further, if someone visited Andrea and saw an interesting book that he wanted to read and asked if he could borrow it, well, of course Andrea would want to say yes. Wouldn't I? There was no greater flattery than having someone peruse your bookshelf and say, "I've always wanted to read The Poems of Christopher Smart, and here, you have it. What an intelligent person you are." With Aristotelian precision I typed an index to codify and order the random vicissitudes of my history. Looking at my books gave me comfort. I felt as though the folds and quires of my existence were threaded in the tight sews of each title. As long as my books were in order, my life was in order. I inserted a copy into Andrea's *What to do if the Pipes Burst* note-book and slid in a copy with my personal papers packed in my suitcase.

I arrived in China as a replacement in a long line of foreign English teachers who had taught at the University over the course of ten years. I inherited the same apartment which each, in turn, had occupied. There were remnants of their stay: moth-eaten sweaters, half-empty bottles of shampoo, abandoned souvenirs, and books. This was not unexpected, although the sending agency that facilitated my contract informed me I would have the best apartment and in-house materials of all their contracts. Perusing my new home for the next year, I shuddered to think what the other teachers I'd trained with were encountering. Every surface was covered in coal dust, paper peeled from the walls, and there was a dead rat on the kitchen floor. Even the library was in allergy-inducing disarray. After days of cleaning, I set to work restoring order to what, I imagined, was a necessary tool in the lives of my English-major students: the ability (and opportunity) to read a literary text in English.

After wiping off the sooty dust from numerous paperbacks lying in heaps on the floor and scattered across three rickety bookshelves, I marveled at the scarcity of modern fiction. To be sure, there were ample copies of Austen, Twain, Hardy and Dickinson, and innumerable volumes of ESL journals, but few novels from the twentieth century. There were a couple of easy reads by Hemingway and London, and I did find a battered copy of Animal Farm, though the allegory in this setting ironically seemed out of place. Perhaps it was the dust, but the room itself exuded the antiquated odor of a nineteenth century musty parlor. I pulled back the coal-laden curtains to let in some light then found space for the decades-old travel literature, the dog-eared, how-to-be-born-again books, and the outdated magazines. As I sat on the thin, worn carpet with Lu Hua, the third-year student I enlisted to help me, I sneezed.

"Seeing the books in order makes my heart warm," he said.

"It makes my head hurt," I said.

Warm or not, few of my students ever ventured in the library or tried to borrow the texts, dismissively citing a familiarity with them in Chinese translation. Jiang Yi, the brightest in her sophomore class, visited one afternoon and asked what I knew of Freud. Delighted by her provocative questions, I mentioned an English translation of his book in my library.

"I want to know what you have to say," she replied.

Conversation—that's what they really wanted—to talk to another human being about their own thoughts and hear the feedback, expand their language skills, test their ideas. Reading in English, for the sake of story, was secondary and primarily done to increase vocabulary. Nevertheless, when a friend in the States offered to send a few books, I asked Jiang Yi what she would like, and she asked for Alcott's Little Women. Lu Hua asked for anything by Virginia Woolf. When the books arrived two months later, Lu Hua had already completed his paper on Woolf, but Jiang Yi was ecstatic.

"You mean I can stop writing down every word I don't know?" she asked. She had been reading the copy from my library. The campus library, she informed me, did not have many books in English.

"Do you go there much?" I asked, wondering how a language major survived without texts.

"No," she said. "It is too hot in summer and too cold in winter, and too noisy all the time. The librarians sit around and talk and drink tea."

"Where do you go to study, then?" I asked.

"There is a reading room at the top of the hill, behind our dormitory. That is the best place to read," she said.

It was not much of a climb, I discovered. There were trees and paths circling the hillside along with stone benches in brushy clearings. Every few yards were students, standing and swaying, muttering and memorizing their texts. My path led to the rear of a building shaped like an enormous round pagoda with sloping, green-tiled roofs that reached to the sky in a domed pinnacle. Inside the sunlit hall were long wooden tables and chairs filled with students, nearly all of them murmuring as they read from textbooks. But this was not a library. There were no stacks. I stood in the doorway of the foyer listening to the lyrical cadence of the human voices. There was a stairway leading upwards behind me. Perhaps I could glimpse the campus from the top; perhaps I could see beyond it. I cautiously climbed the wooden planks afraid the creaking would draw attention to my plan. It was obvious from the dusty rails that few people ventured to the top. On the third flight, a metal cage door halted my adventure. Piles of decaying tomes were buttressed against the iron slats, their yellowed papers and bindings crumbling from their stacked weight. I stood for long, quiet minutes, unable to decipher any of the Chinese characters. I pondered what secrets they held, what stories they might tell. Why would they be locked behind bars? I felt a great sadness for the books. They were rotting away and no one knew. I climbed back down to the first floor, listening again for the murmurs of the students, for the rustling of the leaves, for the sounds of life as I slipped out. On the ground at my feet were broken shards of the green tiled roof. I picked one up and put it in my pocket.

"For my bookshelf," I muttered, and walked back to my room.

The administration had asked me to teach a Western Civilization class for two semesters so I, too, had urgently requested books from my friend in the States and received the history texts in the same box with Lu Hua and Jiang Yi's books. Until then, the only history text I could find in my apartment library was heavy on dates and weak on culture. It didn't matter, my students assured me; they had studied it all in high school. I struggled through the lessons, relying too heavily on memory, until one morning in class I noticed Li Gang surrounded by his classmates, examining a beautifully bound, American, high school history text. He showed it to me with a triumphant heft of the book over his head.

"Where on earth did you find it?" I asked, incredulous that the book could be in such perfect condition or that he could afford to buy it.

"From the library. They are selling donated books from America. There were many like it, but they are all gone now," he answered, still turning the colorful pages for his classmates.

"But they were donated to go on the library shelves," I protested.

"Yes, but we think the library needs the money more," he said, as the rest of the class laughed in agreement.

Li Gang generously let me use his text for a few weeks until my friend's box arrived. Meanwhile, I discovered a bookstore located above a shop that sold mostly English teaching tapes and an eclectic assortment of modern music. I climbed several flights of stairs, until I reached the fifth floor, which was filled with Chinese literature, philosophy, art books, and shelf after shelf of English language study materials. They also sold just about every novel, in English, already on my dusty bookshelf (except Freud and the religious literature.) Slowly it dawned on me that the tepid Victorian literature fit in nicely with the current political ideology; the stories by Austen, James, and Dickens highlighted the immoral, materialistic societies of Western cultures. These were the books approved by the government.

When Jiang Yi mentioned she'd never seen the paintings of Van Gogh (what did the famous Starry, Starry Night look like, she wanted to know), I invited her and some of her classmates to go with me to the bookstore. The large art books were in the back against a wall, behind a low counter, and guarded by a stern woman with permed hair. She consistently ignored the students until I got her attention by asking in English to see one I felt sure would highlight Van Gogh. I had also spotted one about Texas and excitedly pointed to it as well. The shop lady frowned, but pulled down the coffee-table books with a sigh and stood unbearably close as we turned the pages. Jiang Yi studied the paintings of Van Gogh, Vermeer, Cezanne, and Monet, deciding at last that one of Van Gogh's Sunflowers was her favorite.

"It is so full of hope," she said.

"You should come here again and look at more of the paintings," I suggested.

"The store won't allow you to look unless you are going to buy," she said. "Just one of those books is over three hundred Chinese dollars."

I winced at the thought of my books, neatly shelved in pretty rows at home. Of what use were they, decorating my rooms? The list was still in the suitcase. What importance now was my past? The incunabulum was disintegrating. Something in my well-ordered life was starting to fray.

I read less and less while in China. Perhaps it was the dearth of substantive literature, though I still requested books from the friend who wanted to send them to my students. In truth, I was nearly drowning in a sea of new experiences. Escaping into Western literature only took me further away from the place I was desperate to understand. Instead, I began to write more, filling my last minutes before sleep with scrawled entries in my journal, hungering after my own language, testing ideas in my own voice. I wrote hoping that some day I could make sense out of it all. Each day, I conversed with my students in baby sentences, used elementary English words, attempted to expound on themes I barely understood when I attended university, searched for ways to bridge the ocean of differences between us. I wanted to know their stories, their aspirations, and their fears.

I taught journalism to a class of seniors and of all my students, they were the hardest to penetrate. Unlike the students in other classes, they seemed listless and uninterested in my lessons. Early in the semester, I suggested we put together a newsletter or class paper. We would do articles, reviews, cartoons, and advertisements. It could not be done, they whined; the administration would never allow it. I checked and they were right. So I modified the project and required them to do an interview outside the class with any person of their choice. For practice, I would allow them to interview me.

Their questions were good—How do Chinese students compare to English students? And bad—Do you like Chinese food? They were insightful—Do you consider yourself a warm-hearted person? And silly—What do you wear when you like a boy? But I carefully answered each one honestly, as I had promised. They seemed most shocked that I considered them more courageous than American students because they lived seven to a room, had to take cold showers, and contended with rats in their beds; American students, I told them, would have run home crying for their mothers. But they nodded their approval when I told them I liked short skirts.

I eagerly awaited their papers but was devastated when I began grading the assignment. In every essay was a list of complaints about their foreign teacher. "She is stoic … mean … impervious," they railed. "She insults us by calling us poor." My "slimness" proved I was "strict," my blonde hair indicated I was a "bad actress," and my blue eyes were "like steel." A sweet-faced girl named Chen Li, the class leader, was the most vitriolic of all when she wrote, "She is my enemy." I was shattered. Carefully re-reading each paper, I struggled for perspective. What had I said to engender such anger? What innocent conversation could create such malice? I was a stranger in a strange land and even words were no longer my friends. I fell across my bed, incredulous as I read their articles. And then I cried.

I never returned the papers; I was too wounded to even confront the class. When the students passed me in the halls, they would look the other way or avoid my glance in class. Despite trying to understand, and my internal attempts at forgiveness, I was becoming bitter and disillusioned. Reasoning it was a mistake to stay, I considered abandoning my teaching position during the mid-year break. Homesick, I packed my bags and waited for finals. In the dead of winter, when no other building had heat except my own apartment, I staged the oral exams in my living room. For the journalism class, I chose an easy question to grade their answers for content, vocabulary, diction, and grammar. Chen Li, the class leader, entered first. She sat across from me, nervously tapping a pen on her chilblained fingers.

"You look cold," I said, and she nodded. I decided to dispense with casual talk.

"What do you wish to accomplish in your lifetime?" I asked.

She smiled at the simplicity of my question, then with confidence she answered, "I hope to work someday in public relations."

I bit my lip. That was all it took to re-open the wound. From her file I pulled her essay and laid it on the table between us.

"This is an interesting piece of diplomacy," I said quietly.

But I was not prepared for what came next. Tears welled up in her eyes and dropped on her swollen hands. "I am sorry," she whispered. "I felt regret from the minute I gave it back. We all worked together on our papers. We all agreed to say the same thing." At the sight of her tears, the floodgate of all my hurt broke, and I, too, began to cry. I asked her why they had done this.

"You never smiled at us in class," she said. "We were afraid of you. We thought Americans liked to be direct and honest."

I listened and learned more than I wanted to know that day. I had wanted to believe that I was the good guy; I was the one who had sacrificed a nice existence to help people; I was the bridge-builder. Until then, it was all about me. Now the veil had been torn away, exposing my pride. They did not care about my education, my past, or even my motives. What they needed from their teacher was an accepting smile, a listening ear, and a compassionate voice.

One year was not enough time to find my voice or listen to theirs. I elected to stay in China, not knowing for how long. I permanently relinquished my job to Andrea, found a friend to adopt my collie, gave my cat to my mother, had friends store all my books and belongings, and eventually sold the house I had renovated with an agonizing love. I no longer knew what order or disarray my bookshelves were in. The list stayed in the suitcase. I no longer cared. The Chinese have a saying for taking a blind leap of faith: jumping into the ocean. Once content with the seashells and relics of other people's stories, shying away from the painful permanence of my own, I only skirted the shoreline, afraid of drowning. The lives of my students pulled me in; the grace of Cheng Li's repentance pulled me in.

It no longer mattered where I had come from or how I got there. I could barely guess at where I was going. I miss my house, especially now that I have two children who need a yard to romp in. But I have given them two shelves for their own little books, though they are rarely neatly stacked. Nearby, inside a tiny teapot, is a shard of green tile. My children speak the language of their father with an ease that makes me envious but I love the mystery of deciphering their words. One day, we will go back with them to China, and we will go without a list.

HYMN OF UNGRIEF ALLISON SMYTHE

It is not enough to stumble
into an early March morning and see
through windexed air, spent landscapes
already coaxed back to life, euphoric scents
rising from neglected pots, and railings and dirt
beds all over the city as if all had decided
to report for choir practice with peaches
packed in their lunchboxes

or hear rain pattern the dust and pollen
layering windshields and outdoor tabletops
in the sound of a child's chant, calling
on a sky big enough to pardon our craving
to render us something more than an alka-seltzer
epiphany, more than a quiet percolation of earth-steeped
water in the tracks where feet have dented the wet
grass in the going toward and the leaving

behind. Or that far above the pockmarked surface
road where brake lights stud the dusk and a long
parade of headlights jockey for the next inch
of asphalt while the radio tallies the daily
dead like a scratched forty-five,

a spray of dark birds rides a swell of unseen
surf across the backlit sky
until time holds its breath—

ALLISON SMYTHE

the curbs catch the litter of our unsigned dreams
in a trail of breadcrumbs
and someone turns a light on
and someone turns a cheek
It is not enough,
not enough,
but it is something.

THE WAY A DAY CAN BREAK ALLISON SMYTHE

for Cathy McMillan

After weeks of cold indifference
the sun came out, like a lost friend, the air
tinged with memories of other thawings.
We were younger then. Rare snow limned
the campus and we, unschooled in such
reversals of forecast, abandoned
books for bathing suits just two days later.
We sunned in sudden heat, weightless
as the songs blasting from our portable radios.
We were radiant, buoyed by all we did
not yet know, the skin of the world
still intact like a ripe, unbitten peach. The future
tied with a bow—our best, unopened
present. We gleamed
in scentless sweat, our bodies
dazzling in the sun's brilliance, so bright on our lids
that when we opened our eyes we could see
nothing before us.

Cathy, does your daughter remember
you, only two that first and last time
I saw her? The cells in your womb multiplied
in perverse accounting: your child thrived
inside your dying. Somewhere now
she invents your likeness. I would like to tell
her how we rode around Lubbock with the top
rolled down and *Journey* turned up, how you pointed
at white tipped cotton fields and shouted, *Look,
they're growing wool!*, about our double

ALLISON SMYTHE

date to the Hairy Buffalo party where we discovered
you can't taste Everclear in punch. How we shared
hairstyles and heartbreaks, played
cards and baked cookies, saran wrapped
toilet bowls in the dorm. How you laughed.
That summer we caravaned home
in matching, secondhand Toyotas, glassy days
of skiing on the shimmering lake before evening's
slow surrender. I would like to hand her
those days—to give her you—
before
you carried all you would leave behind.

HUNT THE THIMBLE ALLISON SMYTHE

That game we played as kids:
You're getting warm. . . warmer. . . warmer. . . hot!
maneuvering as if by remote control for the hidden
thing—someone's red sock, lollipop, or secret

note, knowing the hunt was richer than the prize.
It's not so simple now, if it ever was
simple, the universe as we have known it
inflating in theories of everything.

Hints lie everywhere like feathers
in a chicken coop, scattering just as you
bend to pick one up. God, the child's
game, with all his halls of doors.

It started with a word
in a language that never was and every stab
at translation in our currency of morning
and night, of skinned knees and long departures

slants a bit of the original intent and thus complicates
the game. Maybe it's all the concrete under
our feet or that mountains eventually hitchhike
to the sea or that I haven't read every book

not yet written that makes time something that needs
to be found and cut loose from space; perhaps
there is something like light that we have
not yet detected but can't stop looking

ALLISON SMYTHE

for and the one who hid it laughing
because there is always another door
cold... colder... colder
and the hider always has the most fun.

A GAME OF HANGMAN RYAN J. JACK MCDERMOTT

*. . . The very first thing as a measure
retains nothing but the quality of starting, the posture*

*Of a stick figure in a game of hangman. Name the letter
and you have the whole thing out, or at least the starting point,
Otherwise the stick figure begins. It's as comical as this,
and death spelled out against or for us.*

—Joel Gunderson, "The Prolific"

When Judith saw Terence dragging Pastor Bob down the hall, his arms locked behind him, she hurried into Leona's room. The door was wide open. The early morning sun, newly slipped under a passing thunderhead, spread horizontally across Leona's bed. The room seemed brighter than usual, the air lighter. Leona slept peacefully. Except for the empty toast plate, the breakfast was untouched beside her bed. Judith picked up two pictures of great-grandchildren that had fallen to the floor during the struggle, and replaced them on the shelf opposite the bed. She was prepared for an emergency, but instead the room lacked even the usual gravity of age. Maybe Pastor Bob's dementia and Leona's weariness had cancelled each other out.

To be on the safe side, she decided to check Leona's blood sugar. She pricked a toe on the left foot, where the diabetes had cut off almost all feeling. The foot was colder than usual, so she spread another blanket over the large body. Then she felt the right wrist for a pulse. Leona was not sleeping.

* * *

Arrayed as along the road to Golgotha, but in a farce treatment of the passion, along a corridor of too many crosses, yet from gallows not trees, Leona's children hung in various stages of hanging. After all these years, these months, they still had not been cut down. Joan and Roger and Steven—Stevie her baby even—and Thomas (who was no surprise,) and Frank, Harold, Janet, Susan—they had it all spelled out above their whole swaying bodies in stark capital letters. Probably some of them had lost and some had won, but she would never know which was which because if you won, you filled in your own letters, and if you lost, they filled in the letters for you. Some said the finalized word was left as tribute, others as actualized sentence. A sky hung, too, behind them, dark as the slate from which their cryptic epitaphs of white paint shone, so that in the sunlight floodlighting over her shoulder (these late rays on level with the gallows, casting infinite shadows over the rocky waves of arid land) the words floated like attendant angels against the slate-gray cumulus clouds. Only parts of the other children yet remained, or yet had appeared. You might assume their bodies to be carrion picked and carved at by vultures, but in this game you scavenged for your own body parts, accumulating them toward death. Howard, of all people, had only his head in the noose. The incomplete inscription over his head—RTIGI—was much too scant even to begin to speak of life expectancy. It was the blind version of the game, so you had no idea how many letters the final word contained. Jude, on Howard's right, already had nineteen letters above her; only her left foot remained invisible. Why did death, Leona wondered, always come with the left foot? Why not hang the neck last, which would seem more natural, and prevent the protracted asphyxiation while the rest of the body assembled itself? But she knew she wondered in vain because, unlike the paper version of the game, here you couldn't sketch a floating foot; each part must hang suspended from the noose, beginning with the head and working down to the fatal foot.

And then she knew nothing but her being as day broke on her, except maybe for the afterimage of a foot suspended, which, since her cataract surgery had left her permanently seeing through dark gauze, could be the misfiltered apprehension of the water pitcher by her bedside, or the stale bedpan the nurse had not yet removed from the night before. She judged by the grayness of the light that it was morning. With a minute pleasure, a consolation prize, really, she recognized that she had woken in the knowledge that she could not walk. Too often over the past year she had humped her weight to the edge of the bed, only to remember the unhealing break in her femur once she was on the floor trying to decide on the least ostentatious way to call the nurse. Certainly her memory had been eroding gradually for years, but she had found that memory was like granite; only the strata washed over by rivulets of passive disuse or avoidance deteriorated noticeably. She could still recite the entire Jonah ditty. (Among other lines worth a giggle: "God said to Jonah, 'Time to go fishin'!' / And Jonah said, 'Man, I don't do missions.'") And if she had the breath for it, she was certain the fifteen-minute chrysanthemum story would go off without a hitch as well. But ever since she had lost her lovely voice in a stroke two decades ago, Leona didn't like to recite in public, much less on the radio as she had done, and as Stevie tried to persuade her to do again after the stroke. She was still understandable—legible, as she put it—but usually she couldn't bear the contrast between her voice and what she remembered it to be. And what did it use to be? She could hear it back there in a dream, and turned her ear toward it.

But when she got there, there was still only the memory of her voice, now in querulous tones, and the gallows along the road that now resembled the Paint Branch hollow out Murdoch way. It was early spring, the brightest greens filtering a green shade onto her children's faces. (Returning from Vietnam, Howard had said that there was a bit of jungle in these Appalachian hollows, too.) Wisteria, not yet in flower, snaked up the poles of the gallows, and now the gallows themselves were brute scaly vines, and the ground, even the eroded gravel of the road, had become a lawn of deep kudzu, deep—almost purple—green. And there was Stevie, the odd one because he was not born on this road like the rest of them, fated from birth in the aseptic glare of St. Luke's, of their mistaken nine-month sojourn in Columbus, hanged now on the family road in the maternal hollow with "SCHWA" written above his head. Normally she would have kept silent—she wasn't religious by local standards, wasn't political—but she had argued with the officials on this one. "Schwa" wasn't even English. Surely a string of four consonants was illegal! Or at least you deserved another chance, given the level of difficulty. Didn't Jesus have his in three different languages? Despite her protests, she knew that difficulty had nothing to do with it. You weren't allowed to see your own word anyway. As a girl she had observed the progress of the games of her neighbors, expecting to find a clue to her own word, but the dictionary is so large, she realized now, and if two people's words seemed somehow related, it was only the coincidence of a great machine's random choices. Or if there was a pattern there, it would be too complex ever to know. Really, it was a wonder the letters in the blanks even formed real words! Or maybe all words were merely facsimiles of the original epitaphs.

The dawn forced her awake again. Outside her door, which could not remain open, she heard the house waking up. She summoned her silence and directed it to the kitchen, where she knew the nurses would be smoking and having their coffee. She refused to call them, even though her immobility demanded this and her situation in a room at the front of the house seemed to require a loud shout. (Len, across the hall in the other front room, sometimes woke her before dawn with cries for assistance meant to carry to the staff room at the back of the house.) She also would not punish their tardiness by soiling her bed, if she could help it. The alternative method of seizing and maintaining their attention was to cultivate a friendship with one of them, usually a younger member of the staff. Frank, who was still mobile and could watch television, kept abreast of popular culture and the spirit of the age in order to hold conversations with his favorite nurse. The spirit of the age! Leona had seen the spirits of many ages; they visited her in the late afternoon silence, and she had cherished their visits well into her seventies.

But now, on the cusp of ninety, nostalgia had grown dull. The ages, the spirits of them. She could hardly care. She was the jewel of the clock, the rhinestone that knows nothing but moving forward. Or she was a cripple, diabetic, bloated, nearly blind, sweeping a reach across the table for the urine bottle.

Then Nurse Judith opened the door, knocking on her way in.

"Are we awake yet?" She picked up the urine bottle from the linoleum beside the bed.

Leona knew she did not expect a reply. She shut her eyes and obeyed the short commands and gentle gestures that accompanied them. Lift up . . . okay . . . Turning now . . . Help me lift . . . okay now . . . Finished? . . . Pillows: and one, two, lift—okay. Then there was the silence of Janet fetching the breakfast tray, the smell of nicotine as she positioned it.

"Give a holler for Judith when you're done," Judith said, closing the door behind her.

With her fingertips, lightly, Leona inspected the breakfast. A fried egg, toast and some grits . . . and a bowl of stewed tomatoes or apples . . . tomatoes by the smell. She was pleased, though not very hungry. The nurses did the cooking, which was one advantage to the small, cheap assisted-living home. The other was that it was a real house—falling apart, admittedly, on the outside, and in a seedy neighborhood, but partly remodeled on the inside with wall-to-wall carpet, wood paneling, linoleum floors and fluorescent lights. Each bedroom had a unique floor plan and one or two windows. Howard could have afforded a newer facility if she had been willing to share her room, but she had insisted on being alone. She was still happy with the choice, as far as immediate living considerations went, and yet she found herself wishing her door would stay open. If she concentrated, on the rare occasions when the door was propped open, she could make the voices from the television in the sitting room down the hall sound like real people. She tried to imagine what their conversations could mean in the context of a home for the dying. But the door was hung on an incline (the whole house was on an incline), so it swung shut unless you propped it, and who would do that?

On Saturdays a church group came to sing songs and read the Bible. They clustered in the hall outside her closed door. The leader, standing in the sitting room down the hall, would talk in a loud voice, but she could hear it only as a drone. The songs, though, came through clearly from a keyboard right outside the door. Most of their hymns were the kind everybody knew, and she would sing along, careful not to be heard beyond the door. When she sang she did not feel nostalgia because she had never done more than go to church most Sundays like everybody else. And she didn't feel like going to the altar to get born again again. Simply, it felt good. Whereas church had been a distraction then, now on these Saturdays she had the feeling that she could just drop everything—the memories and dead children, the spirits and boredom—and run along with it. "I heard an old, old story, dum da-da da-da in glory. He sought me and he bough-ought me, dum dee dum-dum-dum dee dee." At the very least, it felt good. She did wish, though, that they would open the door a crack.

On the previous Saturday she had heard a low conversation close outside the door. It was during the lull after one of the songs, while the preacher in a loud voice asked for hymn requests.

"You know, Joe died last week," a man's voice said.

"Yes," a woman whispered. "And that lady who sat in the corner—the blind one—she died the week before. It seems like every time we come, somebody dies."

"And on Sunday, too. They were both on Sunday. It makes you wonder."

"Well, I guess it's a good thing. Maybe we help them get ready."

"Yes." The man paused, then chuckled. "Or we're a curse."

"Don't say that."

Then they sang "Amazing Grace" for the second time in a row because Louise, who was the most vocal in the sitting room and controlled the television, insisted that they had not yet sung it.

Leona wondered if it was true that the visitors had some effect on their deaths. She could believe it. Why not? You could never tell if it was a blessing or a curse, or if being able to tell even mattered. In this thought she found a similarity to her dream, an action, a choice that could go both ways, and you never knew which way it would go. Her dream opened up to her like a door, and she entered. She tried to remember further, but found herself outside the dream again. It was a revolving door, with the threshold at the other side sealed off from the rest of the building. Again she entered: a choice, a movement, it could be right or wrong, but either way it moved you in the same direction. Turning toward the threshold, she thought she saw a glimpse of her children, then she swung back away.

Outside yet again, she decided that was enough. The children popped up everywhere now, just as they had seemed to pop out all the time and everywhere for fifteen fertile years. Not that she could have regulated her womb, but as she remembered it, she had tried, intending to have so many kids. A woman and her husband needed the labor—help around the property from the boys, surrogate mothering from the older girls. You couldn't find hired help that would work like your own boys; nobody would get up before dawn and work till after dusk for wages that were no better than the filling station or the WPA paid. Your children worked for their own, which would belong to them when they grew, if they survived their hell-raising and one or two wars, and then they would take care of the folks. But she could have had only one, Howard, and she would still be taken care of and the farm would still have gone in '37—not because Frank, Sr., died, but because the boys wouldn't work it anymore.

Now she had entered, spun through, and saw across the threshold through a narrow crack in the door. The road to the farm began in a steep notch, the vegetation eroded from the flesh of the hillside, which was a deep clay-red orange. Behind the notch, a hollow widened out around a creek that ran year-round from more springs than they could count, some roiling out of broad morasses of quicksand and others that you could plug with a finger for a minute until they sprang out nearby to be plugged by another finger, toe or forehead; with this image she remembered her childhood: a fecund game of Twister. As the hollow rounded out it enclosed a bottom of twelve flat, fertile acres, so that, in early womanhood, she came to think of the notch at the bottom of the stream as a cervix, its orange flesh protecting, withholding, then issuing the wagons of milk and garden vegetables for market. Or now, in old age, it secreted her dream: along the hollow road her children hung crucified—full-grown, but returned to be stillborn.

Leona set her tray on the table beside her. She had eaten only the dry white toast. On the wall to her left the window gave obliquely onto the view of a quiet grassy brick street and, across it, a small warehouse. Between the stillness of the window and the distance of her memory, the silence of the morning knew all that could be removed. First, you sold the house and its contents in exchange for this room. The children had died long before, or had taken themselves from you, and the grandchildren receded in similarity until they became one tow-headed, bowl-cut, dimpled youth against an airbrushed background of water lilies. Next, you closed the door. Then even what was inside the door, you could not see. During the veiled days, when she stared unblinking at the window's bright parallelogram, those parts of the past she neglected obsequiously removed themselves, but even those she blinked to retain were being removed, the silence of those small lights that shined without significance, but shined. She hoped it was enough to know only her constancy, and to search it out among the memories that remained, and in her stillness to know nothing but moving forward. She was the diamond in the hand of the clock. And now her silent knowledge was added to her dreams, where it hardened as plaster in a cast in the aspect of motion in the washed-out rivulets of memory.

She hoped it was Saturday so that the church group would come. By her calculations, it could be Friday or Saturday. Had somebody died yet this week? She often did not hear until weeks later that somebody had died, and lately she had heard of the death of a woman whose residence she had never even been aware of. Entering her dream again, prompted again by the question of the church group's morbid effect, she saw a wall of backlit translucent rectangles dappled with occasional block-cut black letters. It was like the portable, changeable signs of plastic and metal they kept outside the used car lots or along the mountain roads advertising a tent meeting. The letters would fall off, but nobody cared because everybody enjoyed deciphering the leftover words. She remembered her cousin's doll shop, which had lasted three months, with the sign outside that read, until the R fell off, "LITTLE BRITCHES." And the sign for the "God Talk" revival series that said "GO_ TA_ _ : HELL_ CHRISTIANS." *For shame!* She would say this for the sake of her children, then put a hand to her giggling mouth. But the letters and lights in the dream now reminded her more of Wheel of Fortune. The scattered characters were not the survivals of a once-complete word, but steps along the way to completing a word. You chose a letter and either way it got you closer to the end of the game. Either way it was death spelled out, just a question of whether for or against you.

Now the partition at the back of the revolving door opened on a wider perspective, through which she saw, below the letters, first Stevie, then Joan, then the others dangling, staggered like carcasses strung up in a multi-level butchery, below other jazzy, green-glittery light boards with full words spelled out on them. Then, with the flip of an invisible circuit breaker, they were set rotating, suspended from an overhead conveyance that shuddered with their pendulous weight like an overburdened garment-go-round at the dry cleaner's. Her eyes followed Stevie's undersized form into the dim rear of the building (the revolving door finally having swung her completely across the dream's threshold) until it brushed softly through a black hatchway and she was fully within the dream as the corpses and their words promenaded by. FULSOME. BUSHEL. Then Patty still alive and kicking: HIN_ER_. And her own word? Her own word she did not know, but how many children must precede you in death before your word is fulfilled and you come to the end and win or lose or win? Some said that if you spelled out your word before accumulating all your body parts, you went to heaven, otherwise the other place. Yet her children, swinging pendulously from their conveyance, continued to revolve, now in, now out of the black hatchways that hid them in their peculiar limbo, and she knew no more of her word than when she had been a young, free-spirited woman. Go ta hell, Christians. Either way, she suspected that even lying crippled in bed, consenting to the removal of the past, would put a letter up there eventually. Waiting, too, was another beginning. She hoped the church group would come soon so she could make another beginning besides waiting.

Her door swung open. Several seconds later she made out a wide form shuffling into her room.

"Pastor Bob," she said loudly, in order to register in his hearing aids. "Pastor Bob, this isn't your room."

"I've come to minister to you, girl." He was close to the bed now, feeling its edges with his hands to find a comfortable place to sit.

"Pastor Bob. If they find you wandering around again—"

"Shut it, girl, I've come to minister to you through our Lord Jesus."

Leona thought maybe she should call a nurse. She didn't want Pastor Bob to piss on her bed or raise a ruckus like he did sometimes. Every month or so she heard news of him sneaking off to McDonald's or breaking his ribs or getting lost down the block. But he had never visited her before, so she decided his visit was better than waiting, and he was pitiful.

"Well, just hold your bladder."

"You hold your tongue, child. Let's pray. You lead." He settled himself askance on the edge of the bed and tucked his chin even lower than it was already set on his thick neck. Before Leona had a chance to begin her prayer, he commenced his own in a low quick monotone. She felt his hand grasping for hers on the bed sheet, then clutching it so that she was afraid her old bones would break. She listened to his prayer to take her mind off the pain.

"Lord Jesus, we come before Thee not knowing nor how nor why Thou hast placed us here and knowing Thou art gonna get us out and restore us to the faithful leadership of Thy flock, O Jesus, Thou who art the goodshepherd, Thou hast not forsaken Thy servants who have come to baptize Thy children in Thy name only, faithful to Thy commandment in Acts when Thou commanded the first apostles go out unto the Gentiles and make servants of Thy name and Thy name only in all the lands, O Jesus . . ."

He took a breath. Leona felt nervous. This prayer did not belong in her room; it belonged outside her closed door, or behind Pastor Bob's closed door.

". . . and because of that faith which Thou hast freely given me to bestow upon the Gentiles, we pray that Thou wilt pour out Thy Name in baptism upon this Thy servant, trusting that Thou who hast given us Thy Word will not withhold Thy holy Name from us in the true baptismal waters of repentance and new life in Thee, O Lord Jesus, Amen."

He raised his head and edged himself off the bed. His lips kept moving, forming silent words. Leona was afraid he might try to baptize her. She couldn't remember whether she had already been baptized.

"Now we need some water, daughter. Here, now, get in this bathtub." She felt him bending to fiddle with invisible faucets. These elderly people, the way they get sometimes!

"There ain't no bathtub there, Pastor Bob."

"Shut your mouth, girl, and get in here."

"My leg's broke. I can't get out of bed. I don't know how you expect me to get into an invisible bathtub."

Pastor Bob straightened up, but remained hunched. Arms akimbo, he took a deep breath. "Well, we'll just have to sprinkle you. It's not what our Lord would want, but He has grace abundant. Reach me over your water bottle, girl."

"I already been baptized." Leona feared his intensity. Within the context of his hallucinations, his mind was working clearly. He was sharp and decisive. The nurses, she knew, would not approve of his visit. If they walked in now and saw his zealous eyes (though she could not see them, she sensed their burn and flash,) they would, rightly or wrongly, put him in the straightjacket.

"When was that?" he said.

"When I was a child, I think."

"Baby baptism don't mean nothing. I'll bet you can't remember it, can you?"

"Well, I suppose I can," Leona said, trying hard to remember. "It was in a river, I think."

"Which river? How old were you?"

"Well, I must have been about eight." Now that she said it, it seemed likely that she had been baptized in second grade. "Well, it must have been in the Guyandotte."

"The Guyandotte, eh? That's where I did all my baptizin'. The Guyandotte's a good river for baptizin'. Well, yes, didn't I baptize all my children in the Guyandotte? But the Spirit is tellin' me, daughter, that you need the anointment of the Spirit. Is your soul prepared?"

"Well, that I don't know." She was relieved that she wouldn't be baptized a second time. That could be dangerous. But preparation of the soul, it seemed, was something altogether different, perhaps even bigger than baptism. She was the jewel of the clock, always prepared for that which required small preparation.

"Daughter, your soul must be prepared to see our Lord Jesus. He sent his Spirit to prepare you, and whether you like it or not the cup is at your lips and the gates of hell yawn like another much bigger, much hotter cup. The cup at your lips will not be taken away from you. You have to decide, girl, you have to act, and that cauldron of molten brimstone will turn to the sweetest nectar overflowing at the banquet table prepared for you by our Lord."

He spoke like he was preaching a sermon to an audience over her shoulder, sending his soft homiletic swells through her so that she floated on them, undulating up and down.

"Your soul is baptized in Jesus' Name, but let me tell you, daughter, your flesh still wallows in the flames of hell. Don't you feel the taste buds cracklin' on your tongue when it takes the first swallow of that fire? Don't you taste even now the sweetest nectar of God's bubbling brook overflowing in your glass at a table with all the nicest foods spread out before you? The choice is yours, an e-ternal feast or a Satan supper! Any way you look at it, sister, you have to drink, and to drink of the cup of overflowing blessing you have to be pre*pared*."

Leona didn't think she would go to hell, since she had already been baptized, but she could remember nothing about a choice and being prepared. Now the preacher had given voice to the signs and gestures of her dream. She had the feeling, bobbing on the waves of his words, that the same impetus impelled her in and out of her dream by means of the revolving door. As the door, with each revolution, had brought her further into the dream, this speech, with each mounting of a swell, pushed her closer to a shore. She supposed she could prepare for *something*. At the very least, preparation would not be boredom, perhaps not even waiting. It could put the penultimate letter on the board. Pastor Bob had just stopped speaking and his lips were footnoting in silence. After all, she thought, what harm could an anointment do?

"All right, Pastor Bob. Are you sure it won't hurt?"

"It will hurt your evil flesh, sure. It'll kill it right off if you prepare yourself just right." He reached to a shelf and pulled down a canister. As he brought it closer to the bed, she knew by its rounded-off edges that it was her Vaseline.

Pastor Bob put a hand on her head, his lips moved again in silent preface, then, while the fingers of his other hand fiddled with the canister cap, he sent out his low undulations.

"Have mercy on Thy servant, O Lord Jesus. Deliver her from all evil, from all sin, from all trials and tribulations. By Thy resurrection power, by Thy Holy Spirit fire, Thou redeemer of all this tired old world, have mercy on Thy servant's soul and give her Thy peace. Set her free from every bond of that Satan and his devil henchmen. Break and shatter and cleave the chains of her flesh; she's comin' to Thee and Thou'll give her rest; set her free to fly like the angels up to heaven where Thou hast prepared the wedding feast especial for her. Into your hands I commend my daughter. Take her back 'cause she's returning to Thee, O Lord; wash her in the holy font of everlasting; clothe her in her heavenly wedding garments. Let angels circle her roundabout and all Thy saints lay out the welcome mat."

While he said these things over her, Pastor Bob's full hand rested on her forehead. His thin white arm, bared at the elbow, bisected Leona's muted view of her room. The flesh of his hand was soft from disuse, smooth to the point of being untraced by personal print and pattern. All was dermis, from the outer layer to the mammalian skeleton, there being no muscle or fat between the outermost and innermost layers of his flesh. As with her own hands, she doubted whether his still produced and shed dead cells, as if the hands of these aged had already died, but existed now in incorruption, sustained by the rest of the living body. The image of his undead hands presented itself to her just as he mentioned heaven, so that his words snapped in curt insistence: he was speaking of her death. She blinked and listened carefully to the rest of his prayer. Instead of preparing her for death, he seemed to be preparing heaven for her. This was not what she had expected. Preparation, surely, could take place in this life. Really, she wanted to be prepared for life, not death.

Now his hand left her and she heard the distant pop of the Vaseline lid. His thumb pressed moistly on her forehead.

"Wait," she said.

Pastor Bob said impatiently, "They that wait upon the Lord shall renew their strength."

"But that's what I want," she said. "I don't want to die just yet."

"For he has conquered death," the pastor said, and began to slide his thumb down her forehead.

"Fine," she said, "but don't do this if it's gonna kill me. I don't want to be killed just yet."

"I have gone to prepare a place for you."

"I want a place right here."

"Shut your mouth, daughter." He removed his ointmented thumb from her head. "You should be grateful to get out of this place." He wobbled, but stabilized himself against her forehead. "I told you to put that back in your pocket."

Leona latched on to this new hallucination. "Why should I?" She knew she had confused him, so she tried to draw him into this other branching of his thought.

"They don't teach these kids nothing no more."

"If I put it back, will you promise not to anoint me?"

"Dang it, girl, don't you bargain with God!" He was shouting. "You drunk the cup now and there ain't no going back! One way or the other, daughter, that's what the Lord Jesus says, and woe unto ye of the broader paths!"

She heard quick movements outside the door, a sharp crack as the door hit the jamb. She felt his fingers moving on her scalp, grappling. Two nurses were there now and they called down the hall, "Terence! Terence!" They tried to grab him, but he pushed them away. "In the name of Jesus," he shouted. The fingers entwined themselves in her hair. "In the name of Jesus!" His thumb traced a greasy cross on her forehead. Then a large black man grabbed him, pinned his arms behind his back, and dragged him out of the room, slamming the door.

The room was quiet. She thought her scalp would hurt from where he grabbed her hair, but it did not. She reached up, touched her forehead and felt the oiled cross. Hmph. She couldn't blame him, poor man. A cross couldn't do much harm. She felt sleepy. Her bad leg throbbed and she remembered that she had forgotten her medication. She knew that her dream would open up to her completely now. The pills were next to the stewed apples. When she took them she would certainly go to sleep.

She would walk down that road again, back into the converse of the hollow, which was no longer a hollow, but a ridge, where the springs bubbled up and ran along the parched ground, between the stones. Beyond the reaches of cracked earth, across which the crosses cast infinite shadows, the horizon was bruise blue with thunderheads lit by the horizontal sun behind her shoulder. Her children, at their intervals along the road, were blanched against their crosses, their features unspecific like those of characters in a dream. Looking down, she saw that her left leg was invisible; it lacked even the phantom pain or presence of an amputated limb. Her shadow showed her standing on one leg, but she had no trouble balancing. From the head of her shadow, the form of a cross behind her extended down the ridge toward the thunderheads. She knew, as she turned to it, that the cross was her own, that her turn was impossible yet happening, that the jewel, which never knows the time it keeps, was seeing the face of the clock. And above the cross was her word, and into the final blank of the word a "T" was inscribed.

EROTIKOS LOGOS SCOTT CAIRNS

I like how you lean over the book, beginning
your day in such generous expectation.
I like how, just now, you are so nearly smiling.

I almost see it. And your eyes lit from within.

We all have been disappointed in the past. Already
I fear your being disappointed now. So much
will depend, of course, upon your own good offices,

upon your willingness to find something worthy here,

even as you bring (as you *must* bring) something worthy
to the effort. So much of what is worthy wants
two struggling toward agreeable repose, requires

grateful coupling of a willing one with a willing other.

I would like for us to find a way to apprehend
this eros honestly, and find a way to offer eros
as a likely figure for much of what we do worth doing.

HOMESTEADING IN PARADISE SALLY CLARK

The season's tomatoes picked,
ripe, red and heavy as breasts,
die kinder beg to
swim
in the shallow creek
behind the house while
the August sun bakes
their immigrant farm.

But *Muti* knows danger
slithers
in narrow eyes and
angry cotton-mouths
lying in wait,
hungry
for exposed flesh and
seeking vengeance.

Bat-guano powder and
hand-poured lead too
costly to be spent killing
snakes,
and *Vater* in far away fields,
wrestling food from amongst
the thorns and thistles,
his arms bleeding from
tears in his flesh and
blisters on his hands,

the small woman sets aside
her boiling jars

SALLY CLARK

waiting to be filled,
perspiration dripping from
her arms and neck and down
the back of her legs,
absorbed briefly by her
faded cotton skirt, the
colors of her shirt
darkened and bleeding
into her skin.

Shouldering the hoe that
weeds the garden in
diminutive hands,
she clutches up
her skirts and her fears
to walk to the creek bed,
ignoring grass burrs grabbing
at her worn stockings,
spear grass arching
into her ankles.

Swallowing hard,
she sets about
to sever the heads of those
black, evil vipers,
hungry
for her children's lives,
cold blood feeding
the dusty ground,
pungent corpses tossed
onto an open fire,
roasting flesh rising
like incense
to a cloudless sky.

Her task complete, she returns to
the house and works to
preserve the blood-ripe tomatoes

that will feed her family through
the coming winter, pausing
occasionally to listen for
the distant sound of
careless laughter; of
gentle, baptismal splashes
carried
on the quiet, summer breeze.

THREE DAYS TRACI BRIMHALL

Jonah swam laps in the relentless tide
of krill and seawater,
rocking with the slow
breaths of the beast, feeling
him rise and surface, opening
his great hole, exhaling,
releasing fetid air,
and the whispers of prayers.

As cool air rushed in,
his parched throat cried out
with songs of thanksgiving
which echoed in the dark cavern
of the creature's belly.

He wiped his salt-stung eyes
with wrinkled fingertips
and searched the open oval
for the pale wink
of one star,
before heaving back
into the deep, cosmic
heart of the sea.

THE TASTE OF LOT'S WIFE TRACI BRIMHALL

He knew she was gone
but couldn't look back
to see her final form,
never realizing it was her
absence he tasted each time
he was in the ocean,
each tear that crept
to the corner of his mouth,
each drop of sweat he licked
from his daughters' bodies.

IN THIS CONFESSIONAL KEITH WALLIS

Starved of sleeps meal of dreams
the werewolf of reality full-moons with heavy step
into vacant possession of thought.
Catching, red-handed,
a mind making love
to the glossy magnetism of mute bodies
with stapled navels
and screaming, unfulfilled, in the stream
where stepping stones
     silently
          lead
               beneath the torrent.

The bedlam of silence,
its Babled walls torturing the soul
in some third degree burning searchlight
of unwrapped confession,
razors deep into unexplored tendernesses
where breathing cuts to tears.

Confessing fantasycide
I accept a sentence of soul-peace
with a suspended sentence of
the fear of silence.

DAWN BONNIE J. ETHERINGTON

Sunlight entwines
Her golden fingers
Through the thick wild locks of Wind
Her laughing amber eyes
Sparkle mischievously,
Crystal gems in her dazzling face
Warm honey skin, silken smooth
Sunlight dances
Her joyous lips raised in rapture
Caressed gently by
A delicate kiss of breeze
New morning is born
Into a loving embrace.

AT THE REEF ALBERT HALEY

ON THE DAY SHE LOST HER FAITH, Teri Wortham awoke with a line of sunlight falling across her forehead. She remained on her cot, blinking and sweat-free for a change, as the increasing brightness swam in and brought with it a diluted version of jungle, of sky, washing the walls with aqua and saturated greens. Gradually Teri caught hold of the buzz of people drifting up from the valley. Voices of native women came together in a brief snatch of praise song. Lying there listening, the happy communal sound reminded Teri of an orchestra rousing itself into tune before the conductor arrived. This was followed by as close to silence as one ever got in a place of constant insect clicks, bird squawks, and invisible crunches. The people had moved off to chapel. Teri heard something new. Thumps. A honeybee, drunk on pollen, flew up against the screened window. Over and over.

Hurrying, she put on a long dress, the beige one that most successfully disguised both her youth and how thin she had become. It had been a minor item at the ministry team's last Soul Talk, how the Master had once sermonized, "When you fast do not be obvious to men, but only to your Father, who is unseen, and He who sees what is done in secret will reward you." Teri had no long mirror to check herself, but she thought she must look passable. Now go.

At the chapel, hymns were sung with great gusto in the dense native polyphony that made even "I'm Redeemed" sound minor key and at the same time as upbeat as a song at a child's birthday party. The brown skinned people let their lungs loose for a long time beneath the tin roof and then, the acoustic soil prepared, Pastor Ketcherside stepped into the pulpit. He turned pages of the Good Book. He was preaching on Jesus bringing salvation to the woman at the well and the nature of real water, real drink, but Teri mostly heard, "Would you agree, brothers and sisters?" It was a rhetorical device that Teri had lately started noticing, and sitting there on the hard seat, fanning herself with an ink-smeared program, she made a mental tally. Sixteen times. At the hymn of invitation a trio of women walked forward to make individual confessions and, in response to that, prayers arose to the Father. Like clockwork, exactly an hour and forty-five minutes after it started, the service was over. Teri stood in the aisle between the folding chairs and engaged in the usual cheerful palavering combined with ministering to women and children and the handful of men. "What has the Spirit done in your life this week, Rika?" "Lawrence, has God laid anything on your heart since we last spoke?" "How is your witness, Pao?"

Pleasantly winded from the scripture, song, and chat, Teri strolled outside and took a position beside the calling bell with its long rope and thatched cover. She seemed to be enjoying this place where she could catch a bit of breeze coming down from the highest peaks, but the moment lasted longer than expected. At first it felt like almost nothing—a slight falling forward into a possible faint. Then she corrected herself, stood up straight, and it became a knowledge. She was quietly and passively observing as her internal mainmast snapped. Feelings, ideas, a whole tightly tied package of who-I-am's unraveled. Belief in God, creation, the man from Nazareth, winged angels, beautiful seraphs, and the hope of heaven fell out of the young woman. These vanished, gone like the last sail slipping over the horizon of the South Pacific.

Pastor Ketcherside strolled past, leading a little girl by the hand. The dark eyed girl had a crayon streaked paper in hand just like an American Sunday School child. "Are you all right?" Ketcherside stopped before Teri. He held his head in a polite tilt like a host inquiring if the guest has enjoyed her meal.

"Wonderful." Teri hesitated then added, "Praises to Him. It's an awesome day, isn't it? And it was such a great service." Automatically the subdued and pious smile came to her lips, and the pastor nodded.

Inside she was reeling. She supposed she had brought this upon herself by a lack of vigilance. Then she compounded it by not speaking to anyone. Too late. Teri left her station.

Inside the dining hall she filched a yeast roll from where the ladies were preparing a lunch of tender chicken and rice. She charmed a whole bottle of Bayer from the elderly Aussie in the commissary. Back at the women's barracks she wrote a brief note, changed clothes in a flurry, and stuffed her red daypack with passport and other essentials. Then she started down the winding, vined trail that led out of the jungle hills.

Hours later, sweaty, sticky, and bug bitten around the ankles and calves, she threw aside her walking stick and stepped onto the beach. She took off her practical, scoop-soled sandals and marched in the sand. She walked right onto the dock. Clutching her zippered Bible (so they would think they knew who and what she was), she climbed aboard a freighter. The sailors tipped their hats and stared at the pale legs that emerged from her shorts. One put down his scraper and threw a mock salute from up by the bridge. They'd seen this before. At least a three-day journey before this one would be far enough away from what had brought her here. The scraper went back to work. The blade bit against metal and peeled paint. Like the captain said, always stay on top of the rust.

IT'S A SIMPLE BEGINNING. You have faith. You wish to share it with others. At home you speak to sanctuary gatherings, raise funds with a mail-out letter, and add sponsors to the computerized list. You are packaged authentically: Miss Teri Marie Wortham, an upbeat, semi-attractive nineteen-year-old coed from Heartland, USA, who proposes to take along cotton blouses and modest, loose-fitting skirts and, with the latest praise songs on your lips, head out for a soul-saving calendar year. "I feel the Lord has opened a door and wants to bless this ministry." This was Teri's key line, and with her brown hair bobbed short and lipstick stroked on straight she had pronounced it with such firm passion that curious faces looked up from the pews where they had been fiddling with her handout and attached résumé. They smiled at such an exemplary young person. Not like the rest of her generation. My gosh, she was so polite. Did she even have a boyfriend? Most likely, no, because her heart belonged to Jesus, but some day out there in the mission field she would find this blessing, too.

When the presentation was over they came to her with handshakes or hugs, and their scribbled checks. They knew everything about her except what was most important, the thing Teri herself remained ignorant of at that point—that inside her was something besides evangelistic fervor and a desire to follow in the Savior's footsteps. This thing was large and trembling upon the apex of its balance point. What she carried within would not hold. Disappointment, disillusionment? Stubborn confusion? A glowering demon of selfishness? No, when the time came those names did not fit. One could not speak of what it was, only the results. Like a piece of a glacier shearing off, it tumbled with a showy splash. It displaced the water, parted the sea. Then it just lay there, coolly drifting.

AT MARANUHA'S ONLY GENERAL STORE—a run-down, board-floor shack called Brand X Market—she mailed a letter to her parents. ("I've felt led to relocate and do some studying and one-on-one ministry for a few months... Of course, I covet your prayers...") That guilt-filled task out of the way, Teri supplied herself with goods to fill three string bags, and then methodically bicycled the ten kilometers to her place. She passed the petrol station, the walled Catholic mission, and the faux tiki-hut buildings of the Windjammer Resort before the human constructions gave way to the white and blue fantasy of beach and ocean on her right and indulgently green taro fields on the left. Overgrown with weeds and vines, her hut was patched and puckered on the sides, but it only cost twenty American dollars by the week. She stocked the wooden shelves with basics such as milk in a box, Weet-Bix, canned stew, canned soup, canned lamb's tongue, and items to cater to her health, too, like paw-paws, green oranges, bunched bananas. And she had something new to her: Steinlagers in liter size.

Night and day Teri inhaled the flowers and fragrances. Frangipani, bougainvillea, hibiscus, red ginger, salty fish frying. The scents wound through her nostrils and curled down inside. Briefly this stirred what she used to call her "soul," so that she began to feel hope in the old way. If all this were a Psalm, what words and tune might it arouse in young David? Your strong hand rescues me from mine enemies? She picked up the Bible. Then everything that had happened with the Ketchersides returned to her, and the mood was snatched away. She would have to give an account. To her sponsors, the church elders, her parents. Even her grandparents. Religion ran in the family. Her great great grandfather Wortham had been a minister on horseback traveling between far-flung clapboard churches. One of Teri's female ancestors had written a hymn after a great tribulation in her life. Now it was in a Nashville publisher's songbook, translated into over thirty languages, bringing blessings throughout the world.

Teri sagged back onto her lumpy futon. She heard parrots cawing and fluttering in the trees. She turned the other way and watched through mosquito netting a trio of homeless island dogs who slunk forward and licked the torn metal cylinders that were tossed out back after she scooped the nourishment from each. This too was a strange thing to contemplate. How the parrots were beautiful, the dogs so bony and off-putting. Stunning feathered colors lived beside nearly hairless pariahs. A peaceable kingdom? More likely a kingdom in pieces. And here she was. She thought for the first time of what she might say. That she had come to realize that belief was itself a talent, like being athletic or the ability to make money or having intelligence. A person had to have a knack for it. She was so sorry that she had been wrong about herself. She should have known. But they mustn't worry. She fully intended to pay them back for the ticket. She would just need a little time.

A JAPANESE COUPLE CAME TO HONEYMOON at the Windjammer. Teri discovered this when she bicycled to town and turned off by a sign that said PRIVATE: RESORT PROPERTY. She leaned the bike on its side and started down a volcanic rock footpath that ended at a shaded picnic table at the edge of the lagoon. Here she could sit and read and catch the ocean breeze, watch the mostly young, but already wealthy, guests sail catamarans and snorkel. No one charged her with trespassing. There was only the short arm of the law on the easy-come, easy-go island. As she took her place at the table, she saw the two out of her side vision. It was obviously their first morning, and the couple lingered between the amazing white spread of sand and beckoning resort activities. The young man lifted his long-lensed camera. Before he could squeeze off a shot he was almost struck by a bareback rider on a chestnut mare that shot out of the coconut palms, a wall of pulsating flesh headed onto the beach. Teri had seen this before, boys and men materializing out of nowhere. The natives liked to gallop just above the tide line. This rider laughed and slapped the flanks of the horse, causing the animal to turn in a circle and its hooves to throw up spurts of sand, his way of being friendly to the one he had almost run down. "Ho!" Horse and rider galloped off. The young man bent over toward the sand, breathing hard. The girl came to him and patted his back.

The second day they got down to serious beach work. The girl studiously rolled out her mat and lay face down and reached behind and untied her bikini top. The young man, frequently rolling himself like he was on a spit, paged through most of a paperback. In due time, the girl turned over, too, making no attempt to cover herself. The new Teri did not feel compelled to avert her eyes as they both held hands, napped, and behaved with the freedom of those who believe themselves to be unobserved. The sun passed from high to low until it was late afternoon and they were finished. The girl gathered their things and started to wipe sand off herself. She shouted and lowered her sunglasses. A banner of bright, burning red covered her tiny chest.

Sunburned or not, Teri found the couple amusing to watch. And why not? She now fixed her eyes on every form of life: nappy-haired island children in blue school jumpers; barefooted women walking to work at the hotel, wearing long dresses with red hibiscus tucked behind their ears; a crazy man with milky cataracts on his eyes who sat outside the Catholic mission, chiseling lines in the dirt with a machete. Teri couldn't help thinking that for the first time she was truly seeing the very ones she had once come to save.

In the evenings she joined the locals, riding in the bed of right-hand drive pickups along the main narrow road. They made the pilgrimage to Shipwreck Joe's on the backside of the island. The trucks were outfitted with stereos connected to twelve-inch box speakers dumped into the back. As they bounced along, the thundering techno beat passed through Teri's bones. When they finally arrived, she had to make sure she still had her Bible. She carried it more as a back-off statement than anything else. In the dark bar she put it in her lap. Over at the bar a New Zealand woman flirted with the keep. Bottles were rattling and clacking in a haze of smoke and a mix of colonial languages. There was a toothless old man who made it his job to regularly clear the tables by coming around and plunking the beer bottles into cardboard boxes at the customers' feet. The first thing he ever said to Teri was in bad English. It was about a typhoon that hit the island years ago. A ship was driven ashore. Its bow ran right into this bar. The ship had been loaded with Scottish blend whiskey. "And salvation arrived, little girl." The man smiled with his spotted gums. Sometimes he pretended he was going to grab Teri's Bible, a sociable form of harassment, soundtracked with laughter. "What is God doing down there, little girl? God protecting something? No, God is revealing!"

"Stop it," she said, but silently she forgave him. One of his arms was shortened and glazed with scars. It might have been a shark bite or more likely wounds from the long ago Pacific War. As for the other men, she always refused to dance with them. She made sure too that she never let the lines of her clothing slip upwards. She sensed that the dark men with their sour breath and their doughy but firmly strapped together bodies respected her. Enough at least to make sure she always got home.

The boys were another story.

The oldest one was probably pre-pre-teen and the lot of them—five as best she could tell—followed her to the hut. She slammed the door and, dizzy and bloated with warm beer, fell upon the futon. They continued to scratch their nails across the hut sides. This was a prelude to their urinating exuberantly onto the nearest bush. Then they howled and ran down the road. Sometimes they must have run for a whole hour without stopping. Because there they were back. Waking her, shouting, "Missionary, missionary!" They had circled the entire island. Or had they?

One night she decided to take up her flashlight to follow, though at a great distance so that the shouts ahead sounded like a parade moving away. The boys wound through the underbrush alongside the road and slid onto a blade-hacked trail that climbed toward the peaks and bluffs of the interior. "I should go back to bed," Teri thought. The flashlight's beam was like a pencil jabbing at a sea of soft black felt. She was drunker than usual and afraid she might fall and lie in a tangle. But she persisted with her unsteady tracking, facilitated by sound and the dim, shadowed evidence of wet vegetation that had recently been punched aside. Suddenly her light beam grew larger, a plate of brightness that spread as it encountered a solid object.

She brushstroked the skirt of light over the length and breadth of the wall of rock. At first she thought she was seeing things, but she blinked and it was still there: men and animals scratched in outline form, and then the grooves had been painted in to reveal bodies, distorted and stick-like. She could tell that it was an old place from the dim time when volcanoes were still cooling. She leaned forward to glide her hands over—what would Pastor Ketcherside call them? Pagan idols. Tangaroa was at the right of the frieze, a ridiculous, stumpy, hooded warrior. A tree-limb-sized male organ extended from his waist. He was fertility personified, spewing his seeds into the earth.

Teri thought of the boys coming here and leaving the muddy footprints she saw at the base of the rock. Repulsion filled her. She wanted to raise her hand and denounce. Or find someone to argue with. This is manmade. It has no power. It is degrading to all of us. But there was no one to hear her exegete the stones. She was going weak over the entire stretch of her body with what she realized she should have felt from the moment she walked away from Ketcherside and company: fear. She crumpled to her knees. It could have looked to an outsider like she was worshipping the island's crudities, but it was something else. She searched for the flashlight, which had rolled away from her. It was behind a bush. She stretched toward it and it remained just beyond her reach as her eyelids chose that moment to come down. "Oh, I'm out of it," she mumbled.

Somewhere in the distance she heard the boys still shouting, "Missionary, missionary!" This time it sounded different. As if they were invoking two words instead of one. Missing everything, missing everything— She lay on her stomach surrounded by the thick silence of mud. She hoped she would fall asleep or sober up before she felt things crawling over her. She hoped the flashlight batteries lasted.

"Bad. Do not go," the old man said at the bar. "Taboo, Death, Kaput."

"What are you talking about?" She had just told him how lately she had taken to swimming across the lagoon until she reached the reef. Her reward was to teeter on the edge of the coral rocks, staring into the foamy breach where the Pacific penetrated and a cloud of blasted ocean spray filled the air.

The bunched wrinkles on the man's face seemed serious. She looked at where half his arm was like melted candle wax. He acted like he might reach out and touch her with it, but then he backed away. "You have heard," he said and faded into the shadows. For some reason it shook her up, how he behaved as if he knew something beyond basic tourist advice of don't get in over your head. It reminded her of the sheet metal scraps wrapped around the base of the more productive coconut trees to keep large island rats from crawling into them. You didn't have to see the peril itself for it to give you pause. She resolved to at least exercise caution and sobriety as she made future forays.

Today the honeymooners were running their own risk. Naïve and happy, they stood out on the reef in shorts, flip flops, and bright, wrinkled American sloganized t-shirts. They had their snorkeling gear and were looking down into the deepest water. The gap.

At the Windjammer's picnic table Teri put aside the Bible and shaded her eyes. She had a liter of beer that she awkwardly swigged from as she watched. In less than a fortnight the boy and girl had become like people she had known in some other life. Of course, they were not natives, but they reminded her of exactly that in the serenity of their play and how she felt compelled to reach out and minister to them in some way. How to explain this impulse? The misleading sense that she could save someone other than herself. It had all seemed like it would be so easy: preach sermons, sit at campfires and sing songs on the beach, give free inoculations at the clinic, and always offer the invitations to pray the believer's prayer and be born again. But in practice it had felt less like fishing for men than emptying her pockets of spare change. The audience was anxious to drop to its knees and collect the coins, admiring each piece's roundness and metallic solidity with no inkling of its monetary worth. She felt like she had learned a way to sprinkle glitter and captivate children.

"You should speak only what uplifts and edifies," Rich, the assistant mission leader, told Teri one night as they sat in a Soul Talk circle. "I've noticed you developing a critical spirit. You're saying things and asking questions in front of our new, weak brothers and sisters. You may not be completely surrendered and committed. You need to take that to the Father."

The air backed up. They seemed to be breathing the same stale molecules over and over. At these meetings they always spoke "from the heart," but no one had ever been upbraided. Rich was the best looking and most masculine of the mission staff. He had left a life of surfing for Jesus. He could get away with it. The others? They avoided eye contact as if they had just witnessed an unseemly public display.

Mrs. Ketcherside was more gentle. She took Teri aside and whispered, "Dear, I know you're mostly lonely. You thought you might meet someone here or stand out some way. I've seen this before. Being a bottom rung servant can consume you. But there are only six more weeks left. Here's the best plan. Just grit your teeth and do what he wants, okay? And remember all these people who are being saved." Teri had not asked who "he" was. As for the saved?

Now the boy and girl dropped their rubber fins and masks. They leaned together. Snorkeling had been swept from the agenda. Lips pressed against lips in the fractured, flying, salty break. It was so clear to Teri. The way the hands locked, the bodies balanced. He was moment by moment making a special adjustment. Just for her. As the kiss went on, a single kiss, impossibly long, he shifted his weight and placed himself at an awkward angle in the effort. All this so he would not accidentally bump against her tender, burned chest.

"Bless you," Teri said. She watched for what must have been another five minutes. They were kissing, kissing. Foreheads, earlobes, necks. But never did he touch her there. Uncanny, delicate, miraculous. Teri felt teary from the pressure of staring so intently into the brightness. She was tempted to a raise a hand to her forehead to shade her eyes, but she might miss something. She already had. No longer profiled like bodies on an urn, they were moving off in a blur, paddling back toward shore.

Without realizing it, she had come to her feet. Her feet. They were not shod in sandals, but she felt herself overlooking that and moving from the shade onto the glaring sand which was hot enough to make her wince. She let herself go a fraction of an inch above the granules, skimming them like a feather. Her body which had become lighter than words was at the disposal of the sea breeze. She was no bother to anyone this time as she felt herself coming up silently behind the boy and girl who were running up the beach toward their thatched honeymoon cottage beneath the sleepy palms. They were soaked and laughing and hardly to the door before they dumped their gear and began rolling off their clothes. Unencumbered, Teri floated to the window. Inside the room beneath the slow swooping ceiling fan, they were shadows drying each other with towels, then lying down on the stiff bed. Their arms formed a single great circle. They remained on their sides. Then they began—slowly. Yes, slowly; she could never have imagined such slowness. Certainly with the girl's condition it had to be done with great care, his fingers gently operating around the pink, peeling breasts, only brushing them for a brief, icy moment. And if it hurt, he must draw back. But he would always return to her. How could this be? You were the virgin sacrifice set aflame in paradise. Ugly, raw, and undesirable. But you had a lover who did not care. In his eyes you lay on white sheets, not in filth and failure. You were his, his entirely.

There was a whunk and Teri turned. The beer had fallen against a leg of the table. She was still seated on the bench. The beer foamed briefly from the plastic body, then leaked through the table and dripped onto the sand. She looked back to the lagoon. It was pure green-blue mirage bordered by real-looking waves cutting away at the reef. There was no one out there.

SHE BOOKED A BOAT RIDE to the main island. The day after that she was on an international flight home. She could not explain it. She could only hold on to what had been left behind.

Teri looked at her shiny wristwatch, which she was wearing for the first time in months. Five hours from now, the plane would be on the ground. She would hurry from the Jetway to the arrival gate and pull up in front of her parents and the gray-haired elders and their wives. In a rush she'd beat back their ordinary questions. ("How did you get so tan, dear? Are you just about jet-lagged to death?") She'd try to hush them and tell them the news. "Courtesy" was what she had decided it was. They must know how kind and considerate and courteous was the One Who Is Greater. Maybe she could cast it in slogan form, something they were vaguely familiar with. "He honors those who stumble in his name," and, "Hear, oh hear. Some balm is still left." It didn't sound right. They might think it was another vacuous but safe enthusiasm she had committed to memory. The best she could do was to reach in her backpack and bring out the book. She would start turning the tissue-thin pages until she found old King Solomon, son of the sad and lonely, harp-playing David. What a difference a generation could make. They believed in the words of the book, yes? Look here at the Song of Songs. Could there be anything greater than this? He calls her "my love." A mission worker traveling in reverse, she might open up their minds to it.

She glanced at the empty aisle seat beside her, then out the window at the clouds stacked thousands of feet below. Through holes in the sky's cover the sparkling western ocean claimed nearly half of the world. She folded her hands in her lap. She was cocooned in the dull jet engine roar which she gradually became more conscious of. She felt passion wearing off her like a thin silver plating on a spoon. The ocean down there again. They would exercise a normal reflex and think she was babbling and overly excited to be home. She could hear it now: "Land's sake, what is this, Teri? A new interpretation you've stumbled upon?" And there would be chuckling at such an exotic and, for them, impossible notion. All too clear what it really was—an excess of equatorial sun and the cumulative effects of a poorly managed diet. White girl gone to seed in the tropics. This could be cured. They must take her to eat out. "Bet you missed good ol' American food."

Teri studied the call button positioned overhead between two air circulation nozzles. If she stabbed at the little orange button, she would be able to ask the attendant for a pillow. She could lay her head to one side, press her cheek against the soft, white rectangle and slip into dreams. The wave-like risings and collapsings would lead back, always back. You can't just blot out eleven months of your life when you're young. She reached up and hesitated. She shifted her body and placed her feet on the backpack stowed beneath the seat ahead of her. Soon she closed her eyes exactly as she was and allowed her head to tip forward. She did not move again until they were touching down and by then she saw it. She was stretching out her arms to hug them. She was thinking of a hut, a bed on the floor, the traces of light shining through thatch above. A wordless kind of thing. They slid easily into small talk as they strolled down the concourse and out of the terminal into the late afternoon of the New World.

GUTTING HOUSES NICOLE GORDY

gotta move on, dawlin
gotta move on fuh true
its a big little city
with a lotta work to do

When you finally set out to do it, you realize that you had been sleeping in the belly of a being for years. You had dreaded the task like one dreads visiting their mother in a nursing home. You didn't want to see it like this. And now your flesh crawls as you peel wallpaper that is really skin, shedding it like layers off a dead snake. You sweat behind the seal of the gasmask as you hack at drywall, as you rip out carpet. You are gutting the house. As you delve, you discover the little jokes that tragedy wrote—a molded bed with the sheets still perfectly made, a wedding invitation for Sunday, the 28th. You are not amused. The house creaks and moans like a fever patient while you carve out its infection beam by beam, square foot by square foot.

gotta move on, dawlin
gotta move on fuh true

You are gutting a house. When you walk outside to eat a sandwich out of your car, you see that it is one house on a street full of houses, and that it is one street in a city full of streets, all festering with abandonment in the bottom of a filthy sink. Futile seems a mild word then, and you know why you put it off for so long. The house peers back at you with a face half skeletal, with that yellow baptismal collar. You go back in and work until nightfall, but there is no force in your blows and your cleaning lacks conviction. You go home to a room or a trailer or a tent and dream of rising water.

its a big little city
with a lotta work to do

When the alarm cries in the morning, you consider retracting under the covers but finally get up because you don't want to have another dream. You pour lukewarm coffee into a thermos that

GUTTING HOUSES

isn't yours and dress in clothes that don't really fit, and you feel pretty sorry for yourself. Driving over littered streets lined with littered houses, you stop at one in particular with the water mark yea-high and the rooms half gutted. And you trudge up that driveway beset on all sides by your waterlogged former belongings and you enter that dead-belly house, because if anyone's going to tear your mildewed family photos off the wall, it damn well better be you.

RESTORATION OF THE CATHEDRAL DIANNE GARCIA

The spiders' slender anchoring webs pull taut,
and arch across sixteen embossed black stones set down as path.
Each spider's built her web and centering, waits—obedient
to her species' call. Silken cable hangs from cedar branch
to mounds of bramble—to ombre brick—from lemon balm to wild rose,
and back—once comes the dusk their finely-woven wheels suspend
above my neighbor's upright spade and coiled garden hose.
And I—I have broken each anchoring web every early morn,

then spent the noon on aching knees, to pull sod back
and repossess the false face of the weathered stones.

SUNDAY 2005 DIANNE GARCIA

When once 'twas pink now
gauzed and gray and soon—deepest of blues:
away the day.
    A ferry passes through.

    Do you Believe? Were I
    To heaven it'd be this
    Time 'tween day and night, riding the boat with
        ghosts—

    Do I believe? Were you
    To hell it d be when, cracked open egg-shell
           memory falls away

When once 'twas deepest blue now, soft—
Shell pink
the sun mounds and light runs
liquid over horizon's edge—
all rivers wind silver to the sea.

ZUGUNRUHE WM. ANTHONY CONNOLLY

I'vo gridando: pace, pace, pace
    —Petrarch

NO ONE KNOWS WHERE WE ARE.

It's a slight exaggeration, but our new home in Missouri is hard to find; even Sacagawea couldn't have pointed Meriwether Lewis and William Clark our way—in the early 1800s they followed the Missouri River south of here. Our house, not far from the nexus of a state and regional highway, is at the end of a new road, which was carved out of an old forest. The house sits in front of a sloping farmer's field bordered with shelter-belt Evergreen and Sycamore. Out front, across the new street, and down a craggy and hardscrabble embankment is a tea-colored pond where Canada Geese repose as if from a delicate watercolorist's magnificent impasto. The western forest line out front, verdant beyond the water, dips allowing each evening's sunset to be incredibly framed. Town, fifteen minutes away by car, can be seen off to the right and southwest by its sodium-tinted glow rising through cloudless night skies. Our subdivision has a name; several local roads rise and fall through the undulating hills to our door; there are many other houses, with occupants, lining the winding streets of our neighborhood. And yet these coordinates are not enough; no one knows where we are, where we live. Couriers and hired handymen get lost on their way here and call for directions or never arrive. Even GPS, they tell us, cannot help.

Since the 1980s, the concept of getting lost, of not finding your target should have been all but obliterated by the public release of GPS—Global Positioning System—a satellite-based navigation system once reserved solely for military purposes.

Thirty or so satellites circle the globe twice daily transmitting signal information to earth. GPS-enabled receivers take this information and use triangulation to fix positions. Any GPS geek will tell you that, essentially, the receiver compares the time a signal was transmitted by a satellite with the time it was received. The time difference tells the GPS receiver how far away the satellite is. Now, with distance measurements from a few more satellites, the receiver can determine the user's position and display it on the unit's electronic map. Once the user's position has been determined, the GPS unit can calculate other information, such as speed, bearing, track, trip distance, distance to destination, sunrise and sunset time, and more.

And we are not to be found despite the fact that the firmament is alive with sensors.

Parents are watching their daughters sleep, unaware that above them the restless sky is suffused with entities speaking the lingua franca of satellites and starlings. Hundreds of satellites orbit silent tracks around earth. Above the parents and their sleeping children, five billion birds will migrate in annual rite of avian passage descending the length of North America; not all will make the journey.

After work, walking through the brightly-lit campus, cold air descending, I came upon a dead bird. It was still warm. Its neck had been broken probably flying into a window it mistook for open sky. Its plumage was an iridescent blue-green-purple that reminded me of vestments. We take care of the dead. I picked the bird up wary of avian flu by sheathing my hand in a sandwich bag. I carried the bird to a flower bed and placed its limp beauty beneath the limbs of a shrub. I muttered a prayer.

It looked like it was sleeping deeply. We find ourselves in these moments as if pinpointing that epicenter of relative inaccessibility; it is a brief respite from lost bearings, a time of repose in the great chain of being ethereal and eternal.

The frontier explorers of this country were not finding what was lost to them, but what had been long before their time been found by others. She knew the way. Although contentious, some believe Lewis and Clark probably could not have found their most practicable and navigable passage without the help of Sacagawea. It is true she was hired as an interpreter, but it was not the Shoshone language she interpreted, but signs found on the landscape familiar to her people. Today when I get a Sacagawea dollar coin and I'm in an ambling mood, I flip it to point me in the right direction. If her smiling face comes up, Liberty above her hair, In God We Trust aside her sleeping cherub child, I ramble the direction her gaze supposes. Loose and free, I feel as blessed as Toussaint Charbonneau, the French-Canadian fur trader who, it's believed, won Sacagawea in a game of chance. I leave the coin for others—Charbonneau shouldn't be alone in winning chance. This rambling, like a bird's drive to migrate, is in my tribe's chromosomes . . .

Who needs a satellite signal to tell you which way to go when you've got the world around you? What good is it if you don't know where it is you want to go? It might go back to what pre-Socratic philosopher Meno said: "How will you go about finding that thing the nature of which is totally unknown to you?"

How will grace find me if GPS cannot?

There is gypsy blood behind my eyes, psalms

in my soul, and dirt under my fingernails. There is a love of trees off in the distance, on the sloping shelter belt behind my home; their silhouettes emanating strength and majesty—a sanctuary for birds. Farther still and away an expanse of cirrus and viscous blue sky beguiles with its ephemeral constancy. Rivulets of my ancestral blood, actual and make-believe, trickled into the loam of my family tree. Little spadework is required bringing it back from the dead, interned not a generation ago, resurrected through story. That blood—depending on humor—cakes, coagulates, clots and spurts a refulgent flow. We are like some gyrovague on a Pentecostal sojourn, venturing from hedge to hovel hopeful for roots, ultimately heaving a restless scythe. Oral legend, the kind that makes the rounds amid the clatter of clinking pints and spooned coffee mugs, suggests a history of tinkers, but the physical evidence lacks verifiability. It would be too easy to adopt legend as grounds for wanderlust; in fact, that's exactly what I've done for years. I've lost my luggage, so I invent the baggage. Where does this restlessness originate then, if not from a grandparent with well worn hobnail boots? Is it all a defense against permanence, a desire to ascribe romanticism to a haphazard pattern? Is this all about purpose, and memory?

Looking up from my desk, the day lightens. The sky is full of birds in agitated flight; a twittering as the way clears through the trees I am growing so fondly of behind my new home. Yet, no one knows where we are.

Birds and trees: God's sublime metaphors, wrought in stark contrast between moving and staying, between nesting and waving in the invisible wind. One eats the light, the other soars through it, borne upon it. Shadows cast from the sentinel, marking time upon the landscape, while the others skitter and slide across the sacred geography of what lies underfoot. Neither can I emulate, neither do I negate these creations great towering, small and alighting. Each contributes to the day's debut: One lifts the veil of dawn with its fingers, while the other sings its praises with throaty warble. This you see as a child, this you recall when you're older, when you're able to gives names to the wonder.

As a child I hid in the trees, using their sanctuary to erect thicket forts for smoking cigarettes or stealing "French" kisses or building surveillance outposts in the latest war against conjured combatants. As a child I would spend endless hours outdoors, beneath trees, on my back cataloguing for an imaginary entomology journal or a dissertation on cloud formation, still ignorant of what the firmament held. On my back, leaning against some ancient oak or supported by an amiable bramble wall, I would watch birds swoop and soar; flying incredibly high or insanely low, seemingly snagged in the tree limbs intersecting my view. The saddest moment was to stumble upon a grounded bird, dead, or find an abandoned nest, eggs cracked and ruined. Scarred trees and burnt fields of grass could produce melancholy, too—the dour Scotch in me—made all the more horrid by the stench caught in my flaring nostrils. Wretched trees caught my stunned attention, bereft of leaves, brittle, yet standing with massive trunks bearing a gouge from malicious axe or wayward car. These numerous accidental signposts spoke in a language without words or voice. The scream could be heard in your knees. These trees were headstones, bark ripped engraving their passing. Even years later, the scar remains—an exposure. Count the rings.

Holding a bird in your hand, you count the breaths. Holding a bird in your hand is akin to cupping light. Everything tells you it won't last. That this is grace, when the wings twitch and the texture of tiny bone and feather brush your palm, alien and delightful. Then, with a sleight bend of the knees, a spring from the waist, arms widening, hands opening, you set that bird free and feel a hitherto unimaginable rush of glory.

It is no surprise that one of the most beautiful sights is finding the bird, a bird, birds, in the limb of a tree. It's all there: The wanting to stay, the urge for flight: Singing, rooting, observing—convocation. Nothing more can be done, but to lean against the massive trunk and sigh, while birds twitter around the branches as if having bathed in Red Bull.

I attest to the allure of caffeine, which clearly has been shown to bring about not only euphoria and clarity, but restlessness: The Joe Jitters of Starbucks' St. Vitus Dance. In my kaffeeklatsch, I have Pascal and Petrarch. Pascal says the human condition is to be found here in equals parts, "inconstance, ennui and inquietude." Boredom and restlessness are so close, as to be affection, an addiction, it has been said. It is the discordance of one's patterns that might be warranted or sought after in a bid to disrupt the incessant march of time. My morning coffee is an animalistic habit part addiction, which sluices into affection the more I consume. Habit doesn't always propel me forward, there are times when conditions present themselves and my soul reacts with a shifting and a reaching. Petrarch spent his life in "restless peregrination," says Eric Ormsby, and expressed this turmoil in his 128th poem: "I'vo gridando: pace, pace, pace," he wrote. "I go my way imploring: peace, peace, peace." It's as if I sip my coffee saying to myself, "calm, calm, calm," when the exact opposite is coursing through my veins. For me is coffee not congruity's hemlock. Still those birds . . .

The time travel book is open, as it was yesterday, as it will be the day after tomorrow, as all rivers run to the sea. There is no remembrance of former things . . . Yet, it is always there on my moaning shelf with Heidegger and Jesus. The Alpha and The Omega is ordered through moods, understanding and speech. . . .neither shall there be any remembrance of things that are to come . . . How do we reconcile Herodotus and Hawking when we sit around the fire telling our stories? What of that lamenting Ecclesiastes preacher? Resignation comes after wisdom, but before songs of love. A time to cast away stones. Before songs of love I must resign myself to the fact there is no possibility of time travel, that all journeys come to an end.

If time travel were possible, I would revisit all the times of insights avoiding all the moments of denial. I'd go back to move the stone; I would return to see the fish; I would return to shoo the birds from the scattered seeds. *Semen est verbum Dei; sator autem Christus*[1]. I would sit with my brother and point out the way across the water: Uncertainty, chaos, but mostly being there for a time guiding each other through the darkness to the known light.

Staring out the window, a comet screams

across the dawn through cracks and panes, looking for a home.

Stardust, a NASA satellite, landed in the Utah desert recently returning with it a tiny payload—less than a teaspoon of comet dust collected in a receptacle covered in aerogel—a spun-glass like substance. (Aerogel looks like blue smoke, it is the world's lightest substance, but can withstand extremes in temperature.) The dust snared in the spun-glass will be analyzed to investigate nothing less than the origins of the universe. In a comet's dust a time frame can be established, for the hanging of the stars, the alignment of planets, the sowing of dark matter. And the comet continues its path toward a home in yonder fields of furrows and hope.

Nearby, on the footpath, skittering swallows peck the well-worn route clean. Beyond this path, the shallow ground sprouts a weak crop easily destroyed by the onslaught of elements. Further still away from the exposed landscape of stone, desperate seedlings struggle for air wending amongst the thorns, gasping and sputtering; wheezing. In the open loam, well tilled and aerated, up rises strong stock soaking in the sun's brilliant rays, the sky's Aegean fugue of seemingly spun glass. Peace be still. Bending and collecting in our palms that which is justified, sanctified, and glorified: abundant grace. It is an attempt at personal theology and it falls short.

Theology beats a narrative heart. Ask Buechner, ask Tillich, asked Saint Augustine. Ask anyone working out a system of belief and behind it will be story. Those trees, those birds. A bridge perhaps.

These are all private, unreliable moments now. You can't tell every one of the gifts laid at your feet. They wouldn't believe it. They are ultimately without interest because it's not their own lives being played out. But if the Bible, if personal theology is nothing, it is a burning light and the evanescence it sheds is a pattern of footsteps, fractals and a certain sangfroidness. For who am I? I know only that I move; body and memory move, from being there to being here inside my heart. I am everything that turns, all apiece mostly, ignorant of being called and invited—deaf, stricken dumb. I am where I'm found. Free to fly; raiment on my back; whose blood and kin were granted passage on a voyage through the greatest of floods; the very same waters bestowed for succor and cleansing, said a deranged man who walked about unshod. Saint Francis said, "God feedeth you, and giveth you the streams and fountains for your drink; the mountains and valleys for your refuge and the high trees whereon to make your nests; and because ye know not how to spin or sow." This is my story, this inability to spin or sow, to clearly understand where my footfalls should match His and where the trail wanders in paths bereft of seed. But then the only way over is through. "Only through the seven virtues is the sevenfold bliss obtained," said Elémaire Zolla.

In those trees something is snared.

There is a term for a period before bird migrates[2]; their formation and grouping is an organic, instinctual order of the highest beauty and intent. *Zugunruhe*: It begins deep in their bones. A need to shift, to move—and leave. To join others and set course. To move temporarily as one. I'm no bird expert. (One summer I played Daddy to a family of precarious warblers who'd fallen prey to my outdoor cats. My action led to their death, but it was not without trying to help the birds.) There appears to be no leader when they migrate, although someone, perhaps alternatively, will take the lead point. The others follow in not a gesture of capitulation, but out of what might be called righteousness. It is the right thing to do.

It is not only right; it's the law. Science, of the kind sans agar-agar and petri dishes, suggests it is a law of nature to seek change and that change is only possible if the conditions are right, if there is incubation with others, if only we organize ourselves into systems and patterns of support. Margaret J. Wheatley and Myron Kellner-Rodgers, in their book *A Simpler Way*, note that to organize is to thrive. Organization, support, allows for growth and creativity. We must organize so that we can change, to not seek change is to stagnate and with static comes eventual death. ". . . [D]estruction is self-imposed." So perhaps a sense of restlessness is simply the beginning of a new transformational cycle. It harkens the devising of new plans. The parents look upon their sleeping angels and decide; they need to see the sky and the stars.

In this way the flock of birds V their way from a lack to that of plenty. Once this craven appetite is somehow met, they scatter until it is once again time to heed the call. Migration of humans is no different, apparently. Moving companies often collect migration data and recently said that in America, migration, like birds, is south. By moving north, especially in winter, anyone defies nature. But we moved my cats, my dog, my wife and me, with our possessions and a desire to change our style of living. It wasn't that we were unhappy down south, in Texas; we were restless for a life we could truly call our own, or thereabouts. Our moves have been precipitated largely by employment opportunities—first mine and ever since, hers. In total, over a period of decades, we have moved lock, stock, and barrel four times. Not explicably nomadic, but to some unsettling. There is a period between leaving where we've been and being where we are that is not without its quivering and pondering: What am I doing? I use this time getting the house dismantled and reassembled—in this way I avoid too much unproductive dredging of my own backwaters. Fortunately, my employment comes with an abundance of what might appear to be downtime. In this period, I unpack; I orientate the family, biped and quad, to the new environment. Our cats, Jigsaw and Beauregard, are the trickiest, of course.

The cats always take the longest to acclimate. They do it, of course, through their nose. Since we've moved from a place where the cats have reigned supreme for more than five years, the scent in our neighborhood, just being constructed, unnerves them. They scurry low to the ground. They apprehensively sniff the air, outside, their tiny furry heads bobbing. They do not go far. Over the days, and weeks, slowly they spread their scent around the grounds and begin to smell the familiar in the outdoor accoutrements I place there —garden chairs, welcome mats, cars. Soon they begin to venture farther than I'd like and I whistle for them to return, which they are seemingly only too glad to do. I stare at them at the window pleading to go out or come back in and think of their ancestors: ocelots, puma, lions, tigers. DNA science now tells us that the domestic cat hails from travelers, cats who traversed the Bering Strait, not once, but twice, setting on home based on what they smelled. Our cats are the descendants of puma. We know more or less how Jigsaw and Beauregard's blood made it here.

But what of me and mine? I question this as I unpack box after box, finding the familiar and the long forgotten. One box, dug out from behind a bunch of others because it was labeled in my own hand, a penmanship that clearly comes from an earlier version of myself, I discover a cache of CDs and cassettes. I choose a few of the tapes, cassettes of recorded music arranged in some cartography euphemistically called "mixed tape." The music that exudes from the thin ribbon of tape takes me back to my youth... the ribbon of tape a stream of consciousness, a river we do step into and find at once foreign and familiar. I am riding my ten speed bike through a hot summer's night, earphones over my ears listening to music as I ride, a knapsack on my back and inside this knapsack strapped to my back is a cassette player. It plays the tape that plays now unearthed from a box among boxes. Listening now, hearing it again, it comes to mind as some kind of evidence that I existed, a younger me, riding a bike through the humid night air, moving. I was either moving toward a perceived love or moving away from her. The particular song, a rock in the river or stream, brings this all back. *I'vo gridando: pace, pace, pace...* I play the particular song—"I'm Falling" by The Bluebells—in a way of creating a mantra, a prayer that says: You existed. You exist. You exist. I'm falling forward. I'm falling backwards. I am a wave, a particle, in the state of younger and older.

Cycling. Listening. Unpacking and assembling. Wandering deserts and hardscrabble winterscapes.

It's not rock solid evidence, this musical interlude that sings time and space as one, but it is more than memory alone. The bike is gone; rusted. So is the knapsack; recycled into tennis shoes. The cassette player and its earphones fill a landfill's mulch. The night is gone; stars long buried, that summer has long vanished. My desire for, her name escapes me, has waned but I am here having once been there, and the song in some profound way helps to prove this movement. But of course, it proves it only to me—and my cats, and dog the most loyal of mendicants. Special treats all around. They know me by what I give them. The contents of cardboard boxes, unpacked, do much the same thing: Confirm. *I'vo gridando: pace, pace, pace.*

And yet I can't help feeling like a stranger everywhere I go and whomever I meet, even if the other is me, young, sweat on my hot skin, breathing hard, falling, falling river of summers gone. A stranger, disorientated and sniveling quietly. Alone? Along the trees those birds, my birds, circle in agitation. Zugunruhe: It's an exotic word. It's musical and appropriate. Unpacking boxes should have such a nomenclature. A life in translation should have such a term applied to it. We are restless, inching toward a home that is not here, but beyond the trees.

Alone, iPod dancing like a free man in love with someone long ago gone, but still in my soul. We know that some will make the transmigration while others won't. Beneath the trees, peeking out now from beneath the boughs I see the orange and pink face of my cat—Jigsaw. From this distance, though I can't be sure, I see her face widen in a smile. The birds are saying with their caws: You exist. You exist. You exist.

Sometimes the source of our moving is apparent. We wend the Bering Strait. We peddle the midsummer's night. We pack up the music for another day. We move. Through the streets of my former city I went, day after day, seeking for what I could not say. I found a sign once, only once advertising a bookstore called Strange Land, a bookstore for theology, literature and discovery. Never did find that bookstore again, but perhaps a year later I walked into its new location quite by accident and in there found I was already there sitting with my fellow writers. We'd been there all along, it seems. Then one day we rose. In our new places, we returned to our desks, our toil, our craft—we turned to the books that guide us; we turned to the Bible. We sought to translate on the page what we saw and felt. We turned to see the patterns in the lives of others. The Vs. The crossings. How they begin, how they fulfill their dreams; we saw how they died. We saw that some endings are not terminal, but temporary periods of unpacking from which we again listen for the call and up from our desks we rise. As if in flight. This is what I feel. Zugunruhe, my Lord, a little restiveness in these bones of mercy, wonder and awe. A little vibration. *I'vo gridando: pace, pace, pace . . .*

No one knows where we are, but I know where to look for answers. I carry the psalms in my restless soul.

---

[1] Latin for: *The word of God is a seed and the sower of the seed is Christ*—author unknown.

[2] The author owes a debt of gratitude to Lester L. Short and his seminal work on avian customs and culture entitled The Lives of Birds.

HISTORY IN HER HAIR LISA OHLEN HARRIS

> To see a world in a grain of sand
> And a heaven in a wild flower,
> Hold infinity in the palm of your hand
> And eternity in an hour.
> —William Blake, "Auguries of Innocence"

WAVES CHURN THE SAND, swirling grains through the shallow water, mixing turquoise to blue to gray as water pours and recedes, each grainy wave reaching closer to us. We pull our beach mat up a few yards to the dry sand and settle in to watch the children play.

My nephew, at six, lets the waves wash his feet as he looks out to the Pacific. He doesn't know yet about stinging jellyfish or sharks or riptides—but I wonder if he feels as small, as vulnerable as he looks, standing there with a patch of white sand dusting his brown shoulder. My nephew raises his fists as if in challenge to the mighty sea, and I hear his small, rough voice drift back to me on the wind as he addresses something so much greater than himself.

"You wanna piece of me?"

Beside me, his mother smiles at this bravado, the small smile of a woman who knows what it is to have a son, to watch courage and tenderness juxtaposed, like the perfect contrast of white sand sticking to a small brown shoulder.

Laurie, my eldest, runs up from the water with sand on her fingers, "Mom, check it out. The sand is made of tiny shells all crunched up."

And it is. The sand here at Kailua Beach is fine, powdery. But on my daughter's fingers I see bits of white and gray and opalescent shell, one piece even purple, like the mussel shells I collected on the California beaches of my own childhood. Laurie pulls her hand away and runs again; she is always running, this one. She stands in the surf next to her cousin and bends down to rinse her hands. He says something, looking to Laurie with love and admiration as younger cousins do. But the wind has changed and all I hear is the surf. The ocean will keep the cousins' words to itself.

Sand blows invisibly into my mouth, between my teeth, where even this fine powder crunches, formed as it is from bits of rock and shell. I spit out what I can, not because it is unclean, but because it is unpleasant. Perhaps some of these grains came from the reef that forms breakers on the south side of the beach. When the tide goes out, her waters will pull the sand out and under, tumbling it, returning it to this island or another, ever smaller, ever finer.

I grew up with sand between my teeth and toes. My own parents hailed from Washington State, where the waters of the Olympic Peninsula and Puget Sound are chilled, the beaches rocky, primitive, unbroken even by years of tidewater pounding and churning. Some places, pine trees grow right down to the shoreline.

The sand on my childhood beaches was coarse and patched with black tar from the Santa Barbara oil spills of 1969. An afternoon at the beach left chunks of tar, like black gum stuck to my feet. When we got home from the beach, before we were allowed to go in the house, my father would tell my brother and me to sit on the back porch. Dipping a rag into a can of turpentine, my father softened the tar and washed our feet. He used a product derived from the pine trees of his northwest roots to cleanse our feet from the tar that should have remained under deep sea floors. We were, all of us, young and strong then.

At night I looked out my bedroom window to the flashing lighthouse on Anacapa Island. City lights trickled out to where the moon sometimes laid a reflective path to Anacapa. The beam turned in the lighthouse tower—so slowly. Then it winked at me, and I knew I was not alone. After a day at the beach, skipping flat stones between breakers, I could still feel the surf's memory tug at my body. I wondered if the low tide had pulled one of those flat stones all the way out to the island, where perhaps the lighthouse keeper would pick it up and put it in his pocket. My dreams tugged me out with the tide and carried me across the sea to places I would visit when I had children of my own.

This fine Kailua sand has found its way into my younger daughter's eyes, so we leave everyone at the beach and come back to the beach house. I sit on the toilet lid as my daughter showers and shampoos. Her eye is still red and sore when she finishes showering, but the sand is gone from it. Wrapped in a towel, she snuggles onto my lap here in the steamy bathroom, with trade winds billowing the curtains at the open window. Her hair smells clean, but nestled in the roots I see grains of sand that didn't rinse away with the shampoo.

"You have tiny shells and bits of history in your hair," I whisper to my daughter. Even here in the steamy bathroom, I can hear the surf. I speak quietly to keep the words between just us two.

We sit on the deck, looking out to the beach and waiting for the rest of the family to return. My daughter counts finches flying out from between plumeria blossoms that look like popcorn balls mounted in the trees. Calling this place paradise treads close to the touristy schmaltz that we've avoided by taking a beach house in a residential neighborhood. The sand in my sheets as I go to bed at night, the faint sound of the surf, and the balmy breezes lifting the curtains tug at my memories, pulling me back to another paradise, another life.

My mother and father moved to Ventura County as newlyweds. That first Christmas, they wrote home about the warm breezes and balmy weather. On New

Year's Day, they welcomed 1963 with a walk on the beach—Mom in her Jackie O. sunglasses and scarf. On Valentine's Day they filled their shiny Coleman cooler with ice and drove up the coast for a picnic in Santa Barbara. I was born nine months later, just before their first anniversary there in paradise.

I feel it with them down through time, somehow. Life is good at this moment on the deck, holding my own daughter with history in her hair—just as life was good for my parents when I was born early in November, 1963.

Laurie's back from the beach now, catching geckos with her cousin. She held one on her palm for a brief observation period before releasing it back into the wild. It was a gecko and not a lizard, she told me, because it had wide feet and lay flat to the ground. She wants to release this one in the bedroom of the beach house because she heard her uncle call it a "house gecko."

I'm surprised that the thought of sleeping with a gecko in the room doesn't creep me out. In this place, at this moment, I'm not afraid of crawling things. I like the idea of a fat-fingered gecko finding his way up the wall as I sleep.

Laurie's braids are grainy with sand. I want to tell her, but already she's gone—running again, off with her cousin to release the gecko behind my nightstand. She'll spend the afternoon catching other gentle creatures and picking the plumeria blooms that she will tuck behind her ear for an hour or two. When the blooms wilt, she'll let them fall to the ground or she'll toss them into the wind and watch them parachute away. Today we have no fear of the future, of stinging creatures or riptides, of the currents that will tug and separate us. For this moment, there is only life.

From our second-floor deck, my younger daughter still looks out to the ocean and its islands in the distance. Remembering the lighthouse of my childhood, I ask her what she sees. She shrugs, as if to say, not much.

"Just the ocean, bumping around out there like always," she says.

Warm rain falls, baptizing us in the gentle elements. The ocean bumps around, twining seaweed and sand under her turquoise surface, like always. Caught here in a grain of time, cousins capture geckos and whisper their confidences to the wind. This hour's memory slips into eternity, with tiny bits of shell and history in her hair.

LAKESIDE MASS CLAIRE MCQUERRY

Across the lake a pickup
trails a thread of dust, curling
between two hills that cup the dregs
of today's sunlight like holy water
in their golden palms.

Here, a Eucharist threads
across the weft of evening, and cold
creeps in off the water.
Shadows grow bolder, lengthen
almost to touch
the hem of the priest's robes.

The only warmth in the world:
that one golden smudge
and the truck.
I imagine the driver, a woman,
reaching for the dimpled aluminum
of a soda can, one hand
on the wheel, acrylic nails tapping.
And a little girl beside her who wonders
at the way her eyes and just the tip of her nose
reflect in the cool glass of the window.

Nothing separates us but this
sky, floating on rippled water.

Communion. The hills gather
driver and passenger into their bright
folds until the truck is only a glint
and then nothing. The body of Christ
dissolving on my tongue.

LAST THOUGHTS BRAD FRUHAUFF

When just a child I'd ask God
to keep a list of all the questions
that seemed so important then but that
I knew I would forget:
like who were the dinosaurs, really,
would I have been the same in another age,
or whether someone asked him to create the cosmos
        where what begins must end.
And there were others I can't recall.

In college, knowing better, and
needing to know more, I dreamt
that in that interview there'd be no questions—
no need for speech at all—
but God would sweep his staggering arm
across high Heaven's truescape
and I would know it all in one grand strange and wonderful
moment:—Creation's map or blueprint
extended in the shape of time
(no simple line or circle, but
a sparkling double-helix,
or the transfixing bulging knot
of a protein chain).

Before I die, in survey of
the meager stores of memory, I demure
from once so urgent; look forth instead
with sighs for my true intended,
                      joy,
and pray what's most surprising in that other world, is
how like it is to this.

SATURDAY MORNING BRAD FRUHAUFF

Somewhere between the ads
for yogurt in a tube
and soup you drink like tea
I became obsessed
with the doctrine of God's foreknowing.

WRITING FROM THE INSIDE OUT LUCI SHAW

How often I've heard the comment from people who discover that I offer journal workshops: "Why on earth should I bother to keep a journal? It sounds time-consuming, and I don't have enough time as it is. And what on earth would I write about? My life's pretty ordinary, boring even. I just can't see the point."

The other morning in the supermarket I noticed the T-shirt slogan: "I'm starring in my own soap opera." It reminded me that even those of us who live relatively predictable lives want to feel that our existence is an on-going story, a story with meaning, a story which, though it may be filled with conflict, uncertainty, and utterly mundane activities, will also find significance and resolution. It is a story which is a part (small, perhaps, but real) of God's on-going Creation story.

Most of us would also love to believe that in writing our own story we are placing ourselves in the context of another, much larger, even more dramatic story in which we may play a part, perhaps just a small part, but still meaningful—God's story, His-tory.

For many years I have been writing from the inside out, from my inmost heart, and with what I hope is transparent honesty to what I am feeling and thinking. It has been a transformative process. And more and more I see God's larger, over-arching movement in my life. He is super-intending me. His intentions for me are larger than I can imagine. He is the choreographer of my life dance. It is He who is introducing a sense of purpose and meaning into me, so that no longer does my living seem like a random, chaotic exercise.

My journal has been the medium for much of this realization. As I listen to my own heart, as I listen for God's voice through my writing, I become aware of who I am, in the deepest sense, to God, and to myself.

Entry:

"*I am new for only a day at a time, like the days on my calendar. Or a moment at a time. In a flash the moment is gone, has already grown old and dim—the details fuzzy. I need to capture that moment in its freshness, before its primary insights have evaporated like steam from a wet roof in the sun.*"

Indeterminacy

Two tourists pass in a crowded bus.
The hairs on their bare arms touch,
for a moment meshing and warm,
then not, the door of the bus
already closed with a thud and a hiss,
a fragment in history, a swiftness
receding. That flash-point when
the future brushes against the past—
we notice it only after. Too late.
Now is already over; if
we stop to look, it's gone.

The heart in my chest—in bed
at midnight I shudder to its thump.
A-gain, it repeats, A-gain,
each iambic beat ending at
the instant of assertion. Showing up
only as one in a trail of alpha sparks
tracking through the corridor of
memory's cloud-chamber. Never
on my bus trip will that *again*
happen again.

VERY LITTLE IN THIS WORLD, very little in our lives, is permanent. Yet there is within each of us a need, an indelible impulse, to hold on to the moments of sudden significance, the events of value and importance to us, the idea that comes to life in the Sunday sermon, the striking image or phrase in a book we read or a film we see that makes a connection, helps us to see our lives in a fresh way, from a new angle. If we are writers, we need a way to hold on to the creative image that seems to attract words and ideas to itself that begin to tell a story, or grow into a poem.

Life being what it often is, a series of other people's urgencies to which we must respond without delay, it is all too easy to let the moment fall between the cracks, or slip away in the rush of circumstances. Unless we find a way to hold on to it, to build upon it, to allow its potential to enrich our lives, to effect healthy growth in us as Christians and as human beings made in God's image, it will wither from inattention, much as the seeds, in Jesus's story of the Sower, shriveled and died because they fell on gravel, or were pecked up by scavenger birds before they had a chance to sprout into new growth.

How may we seize each of these singular moments and hold them like jewels in the hand? Can we give ourselves permission to reflect on them, to treasure them, to preserve them from becoming forgotten fragments in our swirling chaos of living, to let them grow and attract to themselves other thoughts and insights? Will we allow ourselves to probe our lives for evidence of God at work in us? Do we have the energy, the resolve, to grasp some embryonic truth and give it time and space to grow like a seed in the furrow of a thoughtful imagination?

"The motivation varies enormously, but the urge is the same. Maybe, at its simplest, journal-writing is a personal way of imposing some kind of permanence or order on the chaos of the world around us."
—Simon Brett, *The Faber Book of Diarie*

OUR LIVES CONTINUALLY PRESENT US with opportunities in which a journal can become a valuable tool for self-awareness and God-awareness. A personal, reflective, consistent journal is like a miniature internal classroom where we can listen to our own hearts, and learn from them.

I have a saying stuck on the side of a metal filing cabinet in my office: "Words matter: Write to learn what you know." A journal is a clinic where we can take our emotional temperature, where our spiritual well-being can be tested and treated, where spiritual or emotional disease can be checked and a healthy diet and exercise regimen begun.

ENTRY:

"My journal isn't just an object to which I contribute. It constantly talks back and gives back to me—a true confidante, a faithful friend."

WHEN WE THINK ABOUT IT, each of us, in our own unique and various ways, attempts to hold on to past events and relationships.

Photo albums, files of notes and letters, bulletin boards with playbills, ticket stubs, award ribbons, pressed leaves and flowers, quotations, mementos, graduation invitations, etc. are all memory markers. Files of business correspondence, either in hard copy or in our computers, are essential ways for us to keep track of decisions and commitments made, relationships being built, problems to be solved. In one sense, most of the art forms such as poetry, painting, photography, musical composition, which rise out of the context of the individual artist's life and reflect his or her insights and images, are also non-systematic forms of journal-keeping.

ENTRY:

"Today, (and it took all day), I organized my photo prints which have been, over the last six months, lying in scattered and growing piles in my office, ever since we moved. I filled nearly two albums with photos of family gatherings, scenery, visitors, all in chronological sequence. This gave me a quite disproportionate sense of satisfaction. Perhaps this mundane task was a symbol of the ordering of my life, to bring it out of chaos and under my control, like catching up on the past in one's journal, holding everything together in place, so that I could see it for what it was. Here was my life in my hands!"

AN INTRODUCTION TO OUR AUTHORS

CHUCK BAKER
BREATH OF WATER
THE THROAT
Poetry

Chuck Baker is an award-winning poet, writer, and editor from Coquitlam, BC, Canada. Hundreds of his articles and poems have appeared in publications such as *SOUL Mag*, *Woman This Month*, *Writer's Digest*, *Writer's Guide to Creativity*, *New York Moves*, *Healthy Living Magazine*, *Roux Magazine*, and many more. His first collection of poetry, *Cross Examinations*, which includes three contest-winning poems, is now available through amazon.com and amazon.ca. His latest e-book, *Get Poetic*, about how to write and sell more of your poetry, is available at www.todaybooks.com. To see what else he's up to, visit him at www.getchuckbaker.tk.

JILL BERGKAMP
SUNDAY SCHOOL LESSON
Editor's Choice, Poetry

Jill Bergkamp lives in Southern Florida with her husband, sons, and cats. In between dodging hurricanes, she attends Florida Atlantic University where she is studying for a degree in English. Her work has appeared in *Alive Now*, *Catapult* and *The Christian Century*, and is forthcoming in *2River View* and *Wicked Alice*. A Great Blue Heron sometimes watches her through the window while she writes.

TRACI BRIMHALL
THE TASTE OF LOT'S WIFE
THREE DAYS
Poetry

Traci is a native Minnesotan who now lives and writes in New York City. She currently attends Sarah Lawrence College where she is earning her MFA in Poetry. Her work has recently appeared in *a-pos-tro-phe*, *kaleidowhirl* and *Tattoo Highway*.

SCOTT CAIRNS
EROTIKOS LOGOS
Poetry

Scott Cairns is the author of six collections of poetry, most recently *Compass of Affection: Poems New & Selected*. His works have been included in *Best Spiritual Writing*, *Best American Spiritual Writing*, *The Pushcart Prize Collection*, and *Upholding Mystery*, among other anthologies. His poetry has appeared in *The Atlantic Monthly*, *The Paris Review*, *The New Republic*, *Poetry*, *Image*, *Spiritus*, *Western Humanities Review*, and others. He is Professor of English and Director of Creative Writing at University of Missouri. He received a Guggenheim Fellowship for 2006. His spiritual memoir, *Short Trip to the Edge*, will be published by HarperSanFrancisco in 2007.

SALLY CLARK
HOMESTEADING
Poetry

Sally Clark lives in Fredericksburg, Texas. Her award-winning poetry has appeared in the 2007 *Texas Poetry Calendar*, *Purpose*, *Releasing Times*, *Frogpond* and *Trusting Him with Your Addicted Child*, an anthology scheduled for publication in 2007. In addition to poetry, Sally has published humor, children's stories and poems, greeting cards and non-fiction for numerous anthologies. She wrote her poem, "Homesteading," after hearing an account of a cousin's pioneer great-grandmother killing water moccasins so her children could swim safely in their ranch's remote Hill Country creek.

WM. ANTHONY CONNOLLY
ZUGUNRUHE
Creative Nonfiction

Wm. Anthony Connolly is a writer living in Columbia, MO with his wife Dyan and Jigsaw the Wonder Cat, Beauregard the Barbarian and Sugar Baby. "Zugunruhe" is an excerpt of his present work, a spiritual memoir of lyric essays entitled *The Eight Leaves*. He teaches English at the University of Missouri-Columbia. Readers and writers can visit Connolly's web site www.anthonyconnolly.com.

AUTHOR BIOS

PEGGY SMITH DUKE
MOURNING
Poetry

Peggy Smith Duke is a poet and writer living in rural Middle Tennessee with her husband, four dogs, three cats, and an intractable horse. She is a retired human resources professional and has been published in newspapers, professional journals, and magazines for 30 years. Her poetry has appeared most recently in *Subtropics*, *The Trunk*, *Muscadine Lines*, *New Verse News*, and *Traveling: An Anthology*. She holds a BS in journalism, an MA in industrial psychology, and a Writer's Loft certificate from Middle Tennessee State University. She earned an Ed.D. with an emphasis in Corporate Learning from Peabody at Vanderbilt University.

BONNIE J. ETHERINGTON
DAWN
Poetry

Bonnie Etherington, a New Zealand citizen, is a young writer who grew up and currently resides in Indonesia. Her writing career is just starting to gain momentum and soon she hopes to study creative writing at Wollongong University, Australia. She had two poems published in anthologies in 2004, including one that won second prize in a competition run by the Poetry Institute of Australia. Lately she has been working on some devotions for the *Extreme Christian Teens* website, among numerous other projects. Bonnie endeavors to use her many cross-cultural experiences to enrich her writing.

DANIEL H. FAIRLY, JR.
TWO SPIRITS
Poetry

Daniel was born and has spent most of his life in Jackson, Mississippi. He graduated cum laude from Belhaven College this past May with a bachelor's degree in philosophy. He minored in English and history. Daniel is currently employed in his father's commercial cleaning business as a supervisor, a job that allows him to sleep late and listen to too much talk radio, Widespread Panic, and Bob Dylan. He will be marrying his best friend and love of his life, Stefanie McClain in January. They have a Boxer named Cooper and attend two different churches, Lakeside Presbyterian and The Journey, mostly because Daniel is ambiguous and indecisive. He loves and appreciates his family very much, and his favorite author is Flannery O'Connor.

IVAN FAUTE
REMOVED FROM HAZEROTH
Fiction

Ivan Faute is a doctoral student in the Program for Writers at the University of Illinois at Chicago. In addition to work forthcoming in *Driftwood: A Literary Journal of Voices from Afar* and *Karamu*, his story "Tragedy as Cake" was chosen as a finalist in the 2006 World's Best Short Short Story Contest and will appear in the 25th anniversary issue of *The Southeast Review*. Apart from writing, he works with artist and theater groups in community development. He is currently at work revising both his first novel and first full-length stage drama.

DIANNE GARCIA
RESTORATION OF THE CATHEDRAL
SUNDAY 2005
Poetry

Dianne Garcia lives and works in Seattle, Washington, and has grown used to the blue of its lakes, rivers, and salt waters, and to the ever-green conifers. She graduated "two generations or more ago" from the University of Washington (where Roethke's greenhouses can still be found) and Seattle University. She only recently has submitted work for publication. She's been published in *Branches Quarterly* and *The Curbside Review*. Her poems often report that small, quiet—and persistent—holy Voice.

KIMBERLY GEORGE
ON CHILDREN, SEWERS, AND DICTATORS
Creative Nonfiction

Kimberly George earned her BA in English from Westmont College. Currently she resides in Seattle,

WA and is pursuing a master's in counseling psychology at Mars Hill Graduate School. When she is not studying, she is dancing, dining on favorite authors, and working for a local homeless shelter. She is also a contributor to the *Burnside Writers Collective*. With words she hopes to cast vision of a world both glorious and broken, stark and exquisite. In the midst of the paradox, she invites a way of seeing where faith stays present with doubt, and any claim of certainty yet collides with mystery.

NICOLE GORDY
GUTTING HOUSES
Poetry

Nicole Gordy is madly in love with her Savior, Jesus, and aspires to reflect that passion in all areas of her life. Since age five, she has had an insatiable desire to write, write more, and write better. Nicole is currently a junior at the University of New Orleans where she is studying English literature and creative writing. A lifetime resident of New Orleans, Nicole has a deep connection and heart for her city, but also looks forward to pursuing foreign missions opportunities. This is Nicole's first "real" publication and she is happy to be associated with *Relief*.

CHAD GUSLER
MORTISE AND TENON
Fiction

Chad Gusler received a BS in Biblical studies and theology from Eastern Mennonite College. In 1998, he received an MA in religious studies from Eastern Mennonite Seminary. His thesis, "Building a Context for Buddhist and Christian Peacemaking: The Kingdom of God, Pratityasamutpada, and Sunyata," has since left him jobless, so Chad is pursuing an MFA in fiction from Seattle Pacific University's creative writing program. He lives in Virginia with his wife Cyndi and their two children.

ALBERT HALEY
AT THE REEF
Fiction

Albert Haley is the author of *Home Ground: Stories of Two Families and the Land* and the novel *Exotic*, winner of the John Irving First Novel Award. His stories have appeared in *The New Yorker*, *The Atlantic Monthly*, *Rolling Stone*, and various literary journals. He earned a B.A. in economics from Yale and an MFA in creative writing from the University of Houston. Since 1997 he has served as writer in residence at Abilene Christian University in Abilene, Texas. He and wife of 23 years, Joyce Haley, have an 8-year-old son, Coleman.

BRITTANY HAMPTON
MORE THAN THE BURN
Poetry

Brittany Hampton grew up in the Southeast of Kentucky in the Appalachian Mountains. She currently lives in Florida with her husband, Joe, who is in the Air Force, but Kentucky will always be home. She recently won The James Still Award for Short Story from the Mountain Heritage Literary Festival. Her fiction can be found in this fall's issue of *Appalachian Heritage*, and her poetry will be appearing in an upcoming issue of *The Pikeville Review*. She is pursuing an MFA in creative writing from Queens University of Charlotte.

LISA OHLEN HARRIS
HISTORY IN HER HAIR
Creative Nonfiction

Lisa writes from Fort Worth, Texas, where she lives with her husband and four daughters. "History in Her Hair" is dedicated to Lisa's sister-in-law, Carolyn, who died in Hawaii last winter. Visit Lisa's website at www.lisaohlenharris.com.

AMBER HARRIS LEICHNER
HOW I EXPLAIN MY RELIGIOUS HISTORY
Poetry

Amber Harris Leichner, a native of Missoula, Montana, received her B.A. in English at Montana State University-Billings and her M.A. in English and women's studies at the University of Nebraska-Lincoln. Currently, she is pursuing her Ph.D. in 20th Century

AUTHOR BIOS

American Literature and women's studies at UNL. She teaches first-year writing, literature, and women's studies courses in UNL's English Department and serves as an editorial assistant for *Prairie Schooner*. Her work will appear in *The Dos Passos Review*, and her chapbook, *Just This Proof*, is forthcoming from Foothills Press.

RYAN J. JACK MCDERMOTT
A GAME OF HANGMAN
Fiction

Ryan J. Jack McDermott lives with his wife, son, and forthcoming child in Virginia wine country. He holds a master's in theological studies from Duke Divinity School and is now pursuing a doctorate in medieval English literature and theory at the University of Virginia. He is the arts editor of *The New Pantagruel* and has published fiction in *Communique* and essays in *The Christian Century* and *Touchstone*.

CLAIRE MCQUERRY
LAKESIDE MASS
Poetry

Claire McQuerry is earning her MFA in poetry from Arizona State University, where she works as an associate editor for the *Hayden's Ferry Review*. Claire was named a 2006 summer fellow by the Virginia Piper Center for Creative Writing and was a recent winner of the Jeanne Lohmann Poetry Prize.

MAUREEN DOYLE MCQUERRY
CONVERSION
HOLLOWS
HOMING PIGEON
Poetry

Maureen McQuerry, a misplaced Californian, lives in Richland, Washington, and works as a gifted education specialist and teacher. She is the author of *Nuclear Legacy, and Student Inquiry*, and her YA fantasy novel, *Wolfproof*, will be released Oct 1, 2006 (Idylls Press). Maureen's collection of poetry, *Wingward*, recently won the New Eden Chapbook Competition and can be found in the 2006, XVI issue of *Ruah*. Her chapbook, *Relentless Light*, is scheduled for publication in April 2007 with Finishing Line Press. Her poems have appeared in many journals including *Smartish Pace*, *The Atlanta Review*, *Southern Review*, and *The North American Review*. She was the MacAuliffe Fellow for WA State in 2000. Her website is found at www.maureenmcquerry.com.

KRISTIN MULHERN NOBLIN
ADVENT
SILENCE
Poetry

Kristin Mulhern Noblin is a graduate of Wheaton College and has been previously published in *Kodon*, Wheaton's literary magazine, and *InPrint*, Imago Dei Community's zine. She currently lives in Portland, Oregon, with her husband Mike and Reggie the Fish. When she is not teaching middle school English, she is busy standing for truth, beauty, freedom, and love. She enjoys road trips, listening to the rain, watching football, playing cribbage, and dancing with her husband.

NANCY J. NORDENSON
NOTHING CAN SEPARATE
Editor's Choice, Creative Nonfiction

Nancy J. Nordenson is the author of *Just Think: Nourish Your Mind to Feed Your Soul* (Baker). A freelance medical writer, she is also a second-year graduate student in Seattle Pacific University's MFA in Creative Writing program. She and her husband live in Minneapolis and have two sons making their way in the world at college and beyond.

JERRY SALYER
SAMHAIN SHUFFLE
Poetry

Jerry Salyer was born in Parkersburg, West Virginia in 1974. He has a B.S. in aeronautics from Miami of Ohio and a master's in liberal arts from St. John's College of Annapolis, Maryland. During his 5 years as a US Navy officer he was deployed to 23 countries in the Middle East, Africa, Europe, and Asia. His print credits include *The Southern Arts Journal, Catholic Men's*

AUTHOR BIOS

Quarterly, and *Hereditas*. His online credits include *MercatorNet* and *The Internet Review of Science Fiction*.

LUCI SHAW
WRITING FROM THE INSIDE OUT
Creative Nonfiction

Luci Shaw is the author of nine volumes of poetry including *What the Light Was Like* (WordFarm, 2006), *Accompanied by Angels* (Eerdmans, 2006), *The Genesis of It All* (Paraclete, 2006), and a non-fiction prose book *The Crime of Living Cautiously* (IVP). She is Writer in Residence at Regent College in Vancouver, B.C. Widely anthologized, her poetry has appeared in *Weavings*, *Image*, *Books & Culture*, *The Christian Century*, *Rock & Sling*, *Radix*, *Crux*, *Stonework*, *Nimble Spirit* and others. For further information, visit www.lucishaw.com.

MICK SILVA
SAFE BOOKS ARE NOT
Forward

Mick Silva spent five years as editor and writer for Focus on the Family Resources before reinventing himself as an acquisitions editor for WaterBrook Multnomah. He is a summer on the skin-tone wheel. Recently, he made the switch from oval-shaped to decidedly-unsafe rectangular frame reading glasses, which really do seem to make him look smarter.

ALLISON SMYTHE
HYMN OF UNGRIEF
THE WAY A DAY CAN BREAK
TO HIDE AND TO SEEK
Poetry

Allison Smythe studied for an MFA in poetry in the University of Houston Creative Writing Program. She runs Ars Graphica, a graphic design firm, with her husband Wayne Leal, a sculptor. They recently moved family and business from Houston to ten acres in rural Missouri. Her work has appeared in *The Gettysburg Review*, the 2007 *Texas Poetry Calendar*, the *RainTown Review*, *Anderbo.com*, *thematthewshouseproject.com*, *TimeSlice: Houston Poetry 2005*, *The Voice*, *Gulf Coast*, and other journals, anthologies and record albums. She will be featured poet in the 2006 Houston Poetry Fest.

MICHAEL SNYDER
ALL HEALED UP
Editor's Choice, Fiction

Michael Snyder is the husband of one very lovely wife, the father of four spirited children, and the owner of one incredibly dumb dog. He (Michael, not the dog) has a useless degree in music composition and arranging from Belmont University in Nashville, TN. He has enjoyed the privilege of winning a few short story contests and his most recent novel is under editorial review at numerous publishers. Also, he's not exactly sure how he feels about referring to himself in third person.

KEITH WALLIS
IN THIS CONFESSIONAL
Poetry

Apart from being engineering designer in Bedfordshire (England), Keith Wallis is an Elder at his church. He is married with two grown up sons and three grandchildren. He has four pamphlets of poetry under his belt and has had graphics and poetry published in a number of small press magazines. He is also a moderator at *ChristianWriters.com* and has a blog: http://wordsculptures-keith.blogspot.com.

EDITOR BIOS

RELIEF'S EDITORS:

KIMBERLY CULBERTSON EDITOR-IN-CHIEF

Kimberly is a writer who found that the type of Christian writing that she was looking to read was difficult to find. She graduated from Bradley University and taught a few years in inner-city Chicago. In theory, she's working on a book about her time there, but in reality, she's pretty busy with this journal.

HEATHER VON DOEHREN ASSISTANT EDITOR

Heather received her bachelor's degree in English and secondary education with a minor in creative writing from Bradley University, home of Illinois Poet Laureate Kevin Stein. Currently, she is finishing her master's degree from the University of Arkansas.

J. MARK BERTRAND FICTION EDITOR

Mark earned his MFA in Creative Writing at the University of Houston. His recent fiction has appeared in *The New Pantagruel* and *Hardluck Stories*. You can visit his personal blog at jmarkbertrand.com, his fiction technique blog *Notes on Craft* at www.jmarkbertrand.com/fictionblog, and his weekly contributions to *The Master's Artist*, a group blog for Christian writers at http://tpr.typepad.com/themastersartist.

KAREN MIEDRICH-LUO CREATIVE NONFICTION EDITOR

Karen is a writer and language coach who lives in Plano, Texas. She has a BA in religion and philosophy from the University of Georgia and a post-graduate English Lit degree from the University of Houston. She was a staff writer for *Vision Magazine* 2002-2005. She also spent three years teaching English, writing, and history at Wuhan University in China where she met and married her husband, Brad. They have two daughters. She is currently writing a collection of essays about China and working on a book about her cross-cultural marriage. You can read her blog at www.miedrich-luo.blogspot.com.

BRAD FRUHAUFF POETRY EDITOR

Brad is a full-time student, part-time instructor, and sometime writer. While working on his Ph.D. in English, he is living in Evanston, IL, with his wife, Katie, and his two cats, to whom he discourses at length about the saints and sinners of contemporary Christian poetry, about the epistemological significance of syntax and punctuation, and of the existential and religious relevance of irony. (You think he's kidding, but just ask.)

BEN "COACH" CULBERTSON TECHNICAL EDITOR

Coach Culbertson, MCDBA, MCSA, MCT, is a Technical Instructor at New Horizons Computer Learning Center of Chicago, specializing in networking, database, and information management. He also consults on dynamic web tecnnologies, graphic design, and ecommerce. In his spare time, he pretends to be a novelist; he recently completed a fourth draft of his book *Coffee Shop Saints*. Since he is not nearly as cool as the other editors of *Relief*, he will probably complete a fifth, sixth, and seventh draft before he submits it to anyone. You can read his blog at www.coachculbertson.com or learn more about the Coffee Shop Saints at www.coffeeshopsaints.com.

New from
SCOTT CAIRNS

Compass of Affection
SCOTT CAIRNS
Poems New and Selected

Hardcover, 180 pages, $25
ISBN: 1-55725-503-2

IN THIS PROVOCATIVE collection, rich with expression and dense with meaning, Scott Cairns expresses an immediate, incarnate theology of God's power and presence in the world. Spanning thirty years and including selections from four of his previous collections, this volume presents the best of Cairns's work — the holy made tangible, love made flesh, and theology performed rather than discussed.

> **"Scott Cairns [is] perhaps the most important and promising religious poet of his generation."**
> -PRAIRIE SCHOONER

> **"Scott Cairns is one of the best poets alive."**
> -ANNIE DILLARD

PARACLETE PRESS

Shop at your bookstore, by phone, or online. Special 25% discount exclusively for Relief readers: Call 1- 800-451-5006 or order at www.paracletepress.com, and use promo code PRrelief.

LUCI SHAW

From Donna Freitas, in *Publishers Weekly*:
"I started sending postcards to a friend many years ago while I was traveling. I would begin each one by saying, 'the light was like this in Texas, or in Iowa, etc.," explained Luci Shaw about the genesis of *What the Light Was Like* (WordFarm, April), one of several recent books of poems, collected when Shaw realized she had a large number of pieces centered around a particular theme.

Shaw's newest collection, *Accompanied by Angels: Poems of the Incarnation* has a story of similar origin, and only became a book after she realized she had accumulated a large number of poems about the incarnation, most of which were sent out during past Advent seasons in her Christmas cards. Shaw knew without hesitation which poem in the collection strikes the most powerful chord. "It's definitely "Mary's Song." I wrote it twenty-five to thirty years ago." Shaw explained that "Mary's Song"—a poem about Mary as a mother cradling her newborn son—has even been set to music by the Norwegian composer, Knut Nystadt, and is performed all over the world.

"These lucid, engaging narratives lyrics of both free and formal verse can serve as devotional lyrics for the devout or as compelling invitations to the seeker. Carefully crafted yet never pretentious or aloof, they bring the sacred close without denying its inexplicable mystery so that, reading them, we too may seem to be accompanied by angels."
—Julia Kasdorf

Accompanied by Angels: Poems of the Incarnation (Eerdmans 2006), 98 pp, $15.00
Available at Amazon.com and Barnes and Noble
Vist Luci's website at www.lucishaw.com

BURNSIDE
WRITERS COLLECTIVE

An online magazine presenting an alternative to franchise faith

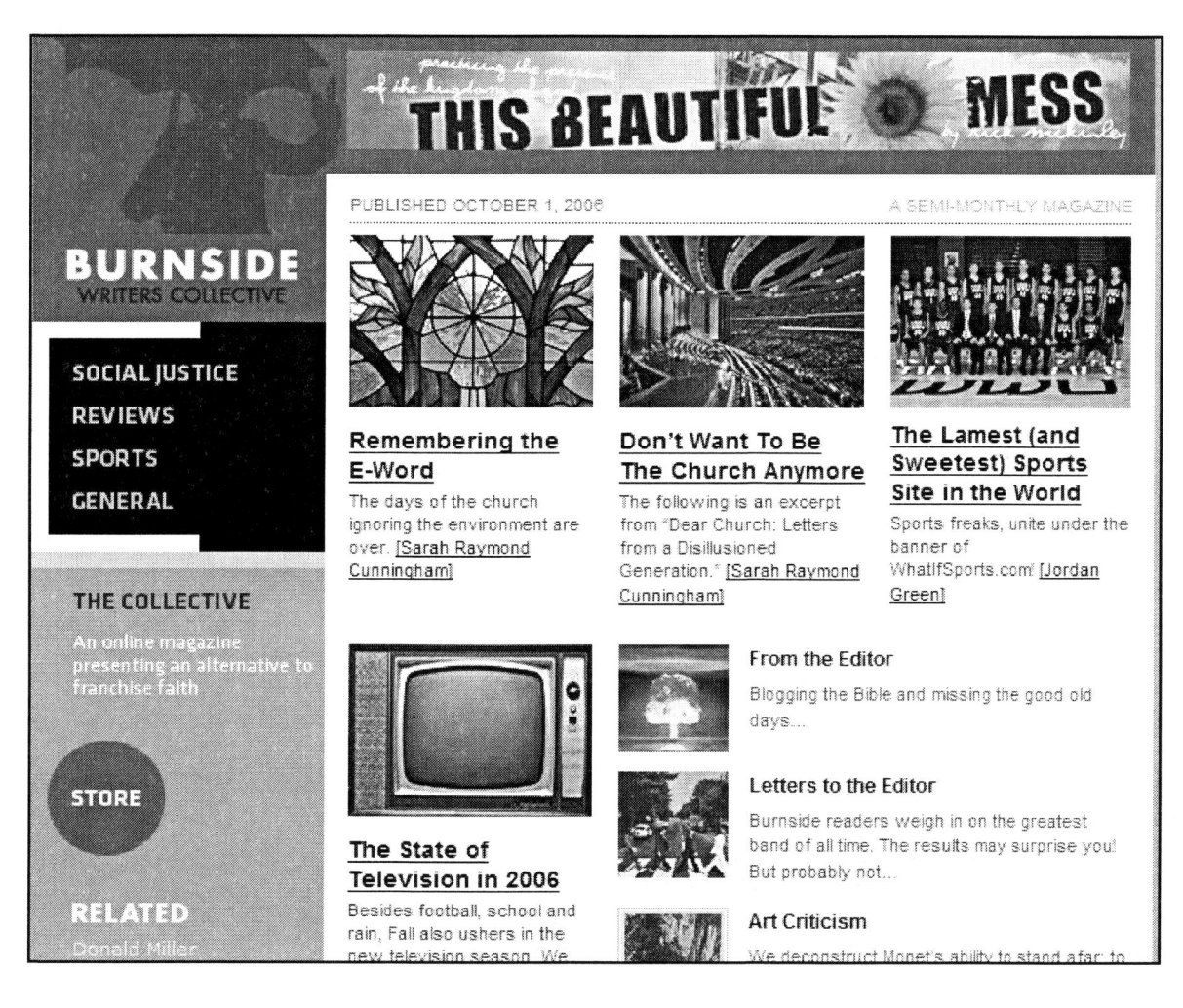

Read it now at
http://www.burnsidewriterscollective.com

Coach,

How about running this response to a literary work we recently published? People might recognize the book, but all I can say is it was an in-house favorite. Many readers told us it was one of the best books they've ever read, and a beautiful exploration of mystery and faith. We anticipated some negative reaction (no conversion scenes), but we believed in the more subtle message about God's work behind the scenes. Anyway, a few responses like this have kept it sitting in the warehouse. It's still available (and we'd welcome any ideas to sell a few more copies), but it isn't likely we'll be working with this fabulous author again any time soon.

Just thought readers might like to know…

--Anonymous Christian Publisher

Subject: [Nuanced Literary Work]
From: Gladys <groach@xxxx>
Date: Tue, 25 Oct 2005 08:22:55 -0700
To: info@Christianpublisher.com

I am a church librarian who completely understands and supports the progressive nature of Christian fiction and how new changes may offend the older generation of more conservative readers. But I would be remiss if I did not write your publishing house after reading the fiction book [Nuanced Literary Work (NLW)].

I purchase for the library your fiction works and enjoy your authors. I thought I would enjoy this since it is a well-known writer. After reading the book, I checked your mission statement. I can only say that [NLW] does not meet your mission. While the writing is very good, this book does absolutely nothing to promote a deeper relationship with God. Even the blurb for the book gives credit for the hope and redemption to the main character rather than God! Your mission says you want to communicate spiritual truth, but this book hints at sex outside marriage (and with a minor in the room!), drinking, as well as ignoring many scriptual (sic) truths like prayer, maintaining a personal relationship with God, and the redemptive work of the savior.

I completely understand I do not need to read this book & should probably just leave it at that since I did enjoy the writing (I am a librarian who has heard every complaint in the world!). At the same time how can I trust your books when this so obviously falls short of your own mission statement? I hope this criticism is taken as constructive. I have trusted your publishing house for quality fiction and I hope my comments are not destructive.

Thanks for your time & consideration.

Sincerely,

Gladys Roach
Changed Name Church Library
Manytown, USA

The Ankeny Briefcase is on it's way. Decemeber 1st. I know a lot of people said that hell would freeze over before it came out, but it looks like they were wrong. Some people say it's the sign of the end of the world. Some people just say that they're glad it's coming out. Some people think it's a unigriff, the offspring of a hippgriff and a unicorn. A lot of people might be angry after they read it. But that's okay. We think it's going to be neat. It's definitely not going to be your typical Guideposts devotional. Not to say that there's anything wrong with Guideposts. Guideposts is great. But Ankeny is just going to be different, that's all. As you can see, the Cardinal here is very staunch in his stance here. What is he so staunch about, anyway? Some stories in the Ankeny Briefcase will use words that some people don't like. But in real life, some people use those words. Is it because they do not have a very large vocabulary? Maybe. Or maybe they grew up in a televisual age in which words have been stripped of their context and no longer mean what they used to mean. Maybe it's just elitism— some people think that people who swear are less than adequate, not suited for high society. Maybe they're right. Maybe we're missing information in our world today because advertisers think people are dumb and sell them stuff based on hype and not quality. Or maybe it's the opposite. I don't know. I wonder if the cardinal on this page knows why. He certainly looks like he does. The cardinal will be on the cover of the Ankeny Briefcase. Perhaps he will share his secrets when it comes out. But probably not. He definitely looks like a proud cardinal. Maybe it's because he knows the secrets of the universe, and knows that if he tells anyone, they won't be secrets, and then he will have nothing to be proud about. But probaby not. He is a very proud cardinal, after all, and he probably has many more things to be proud about. **You'll be able to buy Ankeny Briefcase at http://www.burnsidewriterscollective.com** and also at http://www.reliefjournal.com. **It'll be fifteen bucks.** And the cardinal will be on the cover with that proud but quirky smirk. Neat.

It's not necessarily safe for the whole family...

(Thank God)

Get *Relief* 4 times a year when you subscribe at www.reliefjournal.com. You save $19.76 when you subscribe, because Coach is so crazy, he's going to pay your shipping and handling for you and knock 95 cents off the cover price of each issue! Isn't that neat? We never know what he's going to do next, that crazy Coach.

So why wait? You've just read the first issue and you know you liked it.
Come on, now, don't lie. We know you did.
So point that web browser right over to
www.reliefjournal.com and subscribe today!

ADVERTISEMENT

ANNOUNCING
Coach's Midnight Diner
A Genre Anthology

I'm not all that literary, but I love a good alien ninja story when I find one. Not surprisingly, not many find their way into the Relief submission rounds, but when they do, Kim and Mark tend to let them slip away because they are not looking for genre fiction. Inspired by such submissions to *Relief*, *Coach's Midnight Diner* will showcase cutting edge genre fiction with a Christian slant in the following categories:

Category	Examples (Only for clarification)
*Harboiled Detective/Mystery	*Raymond Chandler, Janet Evanovich
*Horror/Weird Fiction	*H.P. Lovecraft, Stephen King
*Conspiracy/Aliens/Paranormal	*X-Files, Millenium
*Suspense/Adventure	*Dan Brown, James Patterson
*The Fantastic/Archetypal Exploration	*Buffy the Vampire Slayer, Neil Gaiman
*Futurist	*The Twilight Zone, The Outer Limits
*Crime/Police Procedural	*Law and Order, CSI

Combinations of the above genres are welcome and encouraged.

Do not submit:
*Fan Fiction of any kind—We are not going to pay licensing fees or chase down copyright for fan fiction, so don't even think about it. Captain Kirkster or Sculder and Mully stories will be summarily rejected.
*Hardcore Sci-Fi—I'm just not interested in what happened after the Reticulan War on Zeta 3.
*Sword and sorcery—This is not the venue for Elazor and his adventures across the contient of Merminea to save the princess or slay the dragon.

Submission Specs:
Non-Published Short Fiction—10,000 words max. Online Submissions will open December 1, 2006 at http://www.reliefjournal.com. Absolutely no mail-in submissions will be accepted.

Approximate Release Date:
July 2007, pending quality submissions.

Some stories can only be told in an all-night diner after midnight. Here's your chance—the doors are wide open, so go fill up your coffee cup and get to writing. And don't hold back—I'm looking for your best stuff.

—Coach Culbertson, Proprietor

For more information, visit http://www.reliefjournal.com

The following bonus work originally submitted to *Relief* was one of many that inspired *Coach's Midnight Diner*. I'll be sneaking one story in at the end of every issue of *Relief*. "Last Trip to Crystal Moon" is a hardboiled story dealing with a big tatooed bouncer at a strip club who discovers a nasty little secret. Viewer Discretion is advised, but ignore it and enjoy the story.

—Coach Culbertson
Editor, *Coach's Midnight Diner*

LAST TRIP TO CRYSTAL MOON

by R. M. Oliver

"He raped me."

My tongue involuntarily pushes a toothpick around in my mouth as Dana tells me what happened. She is beautiful, despite her already too thick makeup, mixed with tears and dried on her face, despite the dark bruises on her neck. Her tears are spent now and through clenched teeth she tells me what happened, passing her anger to me.

"He must have given me something. I've blacked out before from drinking, but not from two beers." She bites a quivering lip and swears, "heHe left me on the steps outside my apartment."

"Who did this?"

"You know him. His name is Eric, Eric Matthews." Her tone is not accusatory but I feel accused.

You know him... His name is Eric... Eric Matthews.

A huge ball of nausea replaces my stomach. I'd introduced Eric to the club. I wait for an hour in the easy chair next to her bed until she's asleep; then I slip out to the living room. Mike is watching TV with Dana's roommates.

I toss my keys to Mike. "Let's go, dude." Mike will drive because he drives fast. I glance over at Amy, a secretary at a large insurance company, and Tina a nursing student and waitress at the Metro Diner, and wonder how these three women live together.

"Where would a rapist go at a quarter after twelve?" I ask myself out loud as I wait for my gas tank to fill up.

We stop for cigarettes and coffee. Mike guns the truck back onto the road, driving too fast, too aggressive. "Don't get stopped, bro."

You know him... Eric Matthews.

There are not many places Eric would be. We check the gas station where he works, we check his school, his apartment, we even go by the Texas Roadhouse, but he's nowhere.

Mike is getting thirsty, I can tell because he keeps sighing and smoking, and he's still drinking hot coffee at four-thirty when the Texas sun is at its peak.

"You ain't said two words to me all day man." He says after driving around Eric's apartment complex for almost half an hour. "I know what this is about Chris, and I know you're stalling me. Just tell me where this bastard is."

I sigh. "He's at the Crystal Moon."

Mike raises an eyebrow, shrugs, and guns the truck onto I-30.

One year ago Mike was banned for life from the little strip club I work at called the Crystal Moon. Coming through the doors he'd already killed a twelve pack—I knew this because Mike is a non-repentant alcoholic and had been ever since we met in high school. I was on the door that night and he spoke with me for about five minutes before heading to the bar. He ordered two shots, which he drank quickly, and a beer. He picked up the beer and turned around to choose a girl for a lap dance. The moment he left his barstool, another man, equally as inebriated, bumped into him, spilling beer down the front of both of their shirts. Mike didn't say a word; he just dropped his mug and broke the guys nose. I heard the sickening crunch, and saw the spray of blood from the front door and raced over to Mike before any of the other bouncers hurt him. I wasn't fast enough though, and Mike and I ended up in a pile with two other bouncers in front of the mahogany bar. I almost lost my job over that deal, but like I'd done since the day we met, I vouched for Mike. And I explained to him the next morning why he could never come back to the Crystal Moon.

You know him. . . Eric Matthews.

Mike steers the car past an old Chevy pickup clunking along the freeway, and I begin to play the scene out in my mind. I have to take care of this myself, I feel responsible for Eric. I won't call the cops—wouldn't do any good—but it's not like I'm going to reason with the kid, either. I feel like I'm being pounded by remorse, guilt hammering in my head like the six pistons in my truck.

I'd met Eric the day after the incident with Mike. He was a college student who worked at a gas station. One day paying for gas and donuts, I asked how old he was. "Twenty-one in two days."

I spread a thick grin on my face and told him, "I've got just the place for you to celebrate." I gave him a flyer my boss had passed out to all the employees of the Moon.

"You got girls like that?" He indicated a leggy blonde pumping gas outside.

"Better."

I'd convinced myself stripping was harmless fun, just good 'ole boys having a good 'ole time. *Yeah, right, whatever helps you sleep at night.*

In a month Eric was coming in three or four times a week during the day, paling up to my boss, not drinking, but spending all his dough on table dances. I had smiled then, *Harmless—What red blooded American boy doesn't like naked flesh?* At night, when the drinks did flow, Eric would stumble up to me, wanting to spill all the details of his sexual exploits, bragging about how depraved he could be.

Harmless, I'd tell myself, *harmless fun.*

Yeah? Then why do I feel so crappy?

"What's the plan?" Mike snaps me from my haze of memories. He pulls in front of a Mustang, and around an SUV to make our exit. The street name is unimportant because a billboard with a massive arrow hangs over the freeway declaring the delights of the Crystal Moon. He parks at an abandoned fast food restaurant next to the club, and we wait.

It's approaching twilight by the time I see Eric exit the one story building. Mike swings the car around to the front and I'm out and on my feet before the truck is stopped, striding towards Eric.

"Hey Eric," I say. "*Eric.*" He turns around, a big grin on his face. "Where did you get the R?" His smile drops when I mention the date rape drug rhoypnol.

"Where do you think I got it?" He curses.

You know him. . . Eric Matthews.

Dickey Bledsoe is Jabba the Hutt's gray haired big brother, only Dickey is bigger, and walks on two legs, and Jabba was better looking. Well I'm only guessing about two legs because I've never actually seen him walking. He looks ten years older than his forty-nine. Dickey spends all his time at his desk, eating, smoking cheap cigars, and watching the girls on a closed circuit surveillance system he installed when he inherited the club from his aging father.

Two weeks before this incident with Dana, talking to the girls, this sinking in my gut had started, this feeling like I'd eaten a pound of destruction the day I'd agreed to work at the Crystal Moon. My father was not the type to say I told you so but I know he warned me about this.

"He wanted us to come to this 'private party.'" Amanda made the quotation marks with her fingers. "Maybe if I was willing, I could make a lot of money."

"So, you've done private parties before, haven't you?"

"Not like this. We're strippers, Chris, not hookers." Betty said.

"You think he wanted you to. . ."

She closed her eyes and shook her head. "Chris, it was obvious. Dickey is going to ruin this club."

The next day I went in early to talk with him about it.

"What are you implying?" Dickey leaned forward in his chair, his hands on his chin and elbows on the desk forming a triangle, his jowls doubling, his gut spilling over the top of the desk.

"I ain't implying nothing, Dickey. I'm just asking about these parties."

"Just something to pull in some more cash." There was something malicious in his answer, something I knew my father had warned me about. The reek of doom was heavy around Dickey, but I just went home and washed it off, just kept doing my job, kept trying to keep control of overeager and belligerent drunks.

You know him. . . Eric Matthews.

"Ask your boss if you want some R, that's why I sold it to him."

"So you sold him the mickies?"

"I set up a buy for him that's all. I got a finders fee, and a couple lap dances."

"You the one setting up these private parties?"

"Yeah."

"And you need Ruphies to help it along huh?"

"Makes the girls more pliable, right?"

"Right." He nods his head, the look on his face the filth of a thousand rats.

"So you were with Dana last night?"

Eric's smile is Cheshire like and grotesque, he taunts me with a crude gesture. He starts to say something but I cut him off with two quick jabs into his wind, when he doubles over I smash a hard upper cut into his nose, and he crumples to the dirt parking lot. The guy standing on his right lands a good punch to my jaw, but panic blankets him when I shake it off. I grab his arm, pull him close, and head butt him. There's a sharp thwacking of the cranial impact, and he slumps next to Eric. Mike has taken up the slack with the third guy, who is in a pile next to the other two.

"Stay on the ground." I tell them, and I drag Eric to a car and prop him up on it. I squat down close to him. He's dazed so I slap him hard across the mouth.

"You listening to me?"

His head rolls around for a moment and his eyes come clear, focusing on me, pouring out hatred.

I slap him again. "Are you listening?"

"Yes." A trickle of blood has formed at the corner of one of his lips. "Jesus." He says a short prayer.

I speak to him in a whisper so only he and I can hear. I tell him he's banned from the Crystal Moon for life; I make sure he understands the consequences of trying anything like this again. "Leave town. If Mike or I see you around here, you're dead. You understand?"

He starts to mouth off and this time I backhand him. I'm still whispering.

"Are we clear?"

He nods and I put my hand up by my ear and say, "What?"

"Yes, I understand."

"Good."

"Now what?" Mike asks as Eric and his cronies drive away. "I go inside I spend nine weeks in lockup."

"I don't need you to go inside." I retrieve a short, wooden, little league, baseball bat I keep in my truck.

"Dude, what's up?"

"As soon as Betty and Amanda come out call the cops."

He sighs, "Dude, wait—awe damn it—just let it go." He puts his hand on my shoulder but I shrug it away and shake my head no.

"Just make the call -wait around the back for me." I spit on the ground.

He nods and I walk through the front door of the Crystal Moon Gentlemen's Club for the last time.

The anchorman sits ridged in his chair as they always do, delivering the news with a stern or joyful look depending on the story. Now his face is stern. "A local Gentlemen's Club was raided tonight on the anonymous tip that the owner was selling the date rape drug rhoypnol to his customers. The tip, sadly, turned out to be true, as the police found the club empty and the owner tied to his chair and his desk covered with vials of the drug. Susanne Gonzales, the spokeswoman for the special rape and domestic assault division told us of none of the dancers remember who perpetrated this act of vigilantism."

Mike slaps me hard on the back, "I'm proud of you, boy." He swears, "Dickey Bledsoe's finally got what he's had coming."

He's proud of you for letting that kid go free?

I don't feel proud of myself. "I'm tired of this." I say. I should have killed Eric. *And you'd be spending the rest of your sorry life in prison;* I hear my father's voice.

"Tired of what?"

"Always living on the edge of trouble, man. My daddy wouldn't have wanted me to live this way. Before he died he told me it was never too late for a man to change." My beer tastes strangely sour so I set it down on Dana's coffee table. "You believe that?"

Mike drains his beer and twists open a new one. "Maybe, dude. I guess a man has to want to change."

"I feel like I've wanted to change my whole life."

Mike drinks half his beer. "Well, I guess you're half way there then." He chuckles, looking intently at the label on his beer, twisting the bottle around. "You ain't getting all born again on me, are you?"

I thought you were already born again.

"Maybe," I smile. "I wonder if there's a church that needs a big tattooed bouncer."

"Who'd you bounce out of a church?"

"The pastor, I guess if he gets boring, or talks too long."

Mike laughs and finishes his beer. "You want some more?"

I shake my head. "Where would you go if you left here?" I ask Mike.

"I can't leave, bro. I'm tied to this place."

I sigh. "Trapped."

"Naw just stuck man. But that ain't true for you." Mike sucks on his teeth and nods, "What was that girl's name, that one you dated for a while before you went to work at the Moon? Jackie, Jamie, Judy?" He snaps his fingers trying to remember her
name.

"Jennifer. Jen." I say. "She moved back to Texarkana, I think."

"I liked her. She was a real nice girl." He says, standing up. I suppose to fetch another beer.

"I liked her, too." I say as I walk out the front door.

R. M. OLIVER is a drifter by birth that used to wander around as a child making up all sorts of wild adventures. He's currently studying Humanities at The Criswell College in Dallas, Texas. He plans on marrying his amazing girlfriend a year from December. He's been searching for an outlet for his little yarns since he was twelve and is overjoyed to be given this opportunity. He is currently loving philosophy class and is entering his third year teaching ESL to immigrants from Latin America. He dreams of one day owning a Torta y Tacos Restaurant in Huatulco Bay on the Mexican Coast, and being known as the crazy gringo who talks to himself.

Coming soon to ReliefJournal.com:

THE RELIEF ONLINE WRITER'S NETWORK

A unique online community made up of writers dedicated to authentic writing and expression.